ISLAND-IN-WAITING

ISLAND-IN-WAITING

Anthea Fraser

Chivers Press • Thorndike Press
Bath, England   Thorndike, Maine USA

This Large Print edition is published by Chivers Press, England, and by Thorndike Press, USA.

Published in 2000 in the U.K. by arrangement with the author.

Published in 2000 in the U.S. by arrangement with Juliet Burton Literary Agency.

U.K. Hardcover   ISBN 0–7540–3985–4 (Chivers Large Print)
U.K. Softcover   ISBN 0–7540–3986–2 (Camden Large Print)
U.S. Softcover   ISBN 0–7862–2309–X (General Series Edition)

The text of this Large Print edition is unabridged.
Other aspects of the book may vary from the original edition.

Set in 16 pt. New Times Roman.

Printed in Great Britain on acid-free paper.

British Library Cataloguing in Publication Data available

Library of Congress Cataloging-in-Publication Data

Fraser, Anthea.
    Island-in-waiting / c Anthea Fraser.
       p.   cm.
    ISBN 0–7862–2309–X (lg. print : sc : alk. paper)
    1. Young women—Isle of Man—Fiction. 2. Telepathy—
Fiction 3. Isle of Man—Fiction. 4. Large type books. I. Title.
PR6056.R286 I84   2000
823'.914—dc21   99–049386

CHAPTER ONE

Sometimes I wonder how different my life would have been if I had not gone to the theatre that evening five years ago; whether, without the legacy of summoning voice and abnormally vivid dreams, I should still have visited Hugo in the Isle of Man and, once there, become so involved in the fabric of its past. Or were the dreams themselves the gateway to all that lay ahead?

As I waited in the departure lounge at Heathrow, however, I had no suspicion that those dreams would overlap into my waking life and dominate it. I knew only that once again, after barely two weeks at home, I was running away from my parents' exasperation, and wondered dejectedly why I alone of the family should have been denied a share in its brilliance.

For brilliant the rest of them undoubtedly were. My father was Professor of History at one of the Oxford colleges, my mother head of an exclusive girls' school, while brother Hugo, after an outstanding university career, had recently been appointed to the staff of the famous St Olaf's College in the Isle of Man. It was to Hugo I was running now.

'We regret to announce a delay of fifteen minutes in the Isle of Man flight.'

The disembodied voice broke into my musings and I turned my head. It was then that I saw him through the crowd, tall and fair, infinitely reassuring and familiar. I started to my feet with a smile and began to make my way towards him. Then, between one heartbeat and the next, a startling fact slammed into me, bringing me to an abrupt halt. *I hadn't the slightest idea who he was!*

I stood immobile, a rock in the moving sea of people, struggling to tie down my undeniable recognition, and, drawn by the force of my gaze, he turned towards me. His eyes met mine briefly and moved on. Clearly he didn't share my awareness.

Hoping no-one had noticed my discomfiture I returned to my seat and opened the magazine I had bought for the flight while my chaotic thoughts continued to crash into each other.

The recognition had been so instantaneous, so natural and instinctive, that it was impossible to dismiss simply as a mistake. He didn't resemble anyone I knew, nor, I felt sure, was he an actor or politician whose face was known to everyone. It had been a deep, personal familiarity I had felt and started to act on, as though the most natural thing would have been to hurry to him and receive his kiss. I could only thank Providence that reason had reasserted itself before I'd made even more of a fool of myself.

The flight was called and I moved with the crowd into the windy October night and across the tarmac to the waiting plane. He was already seated as I walked down the aisle to my place and as our eyes met the feeling of intimacy again washed over me. It was obviously one-sided. His own glance held only the guarded appreciation of any man face to face with any reasonably attractive girl.

The incident had disturbed me considerably and as I fumbled with the seat-belt I was trying to regain some measure of calm. After all, no harm was done; he was quite unaware of my narrowly averted *faux pas*.

'Just relax, dear,' advised a motherly voice on my right. 'No need to feel nervous.'

I turned to meet the kindly smile of a middle-aged woman who had taken the seat next to me.

'Thanks, but I'm not worried about the flight.'

'Sorry if I spoke out of turn, I thought you seemed a bit flustered. You're used to all this, are you?'

'Fairly. I flew home from France two weeks ago.'

'Lucky you! Have a nice holiday?'

'Not exactly, it was hard work! I was in Paris for eighteen months on a cookery course and then spent the summer working at a hotel in Provence.'

'Well now, fancy that! Not that I like all that

3

foreign stuff myself, mind. Give me plain English cooking any day. And what are you going to do with yourself now?'

What indeed? It was partly to postpone making such a decision that I had come to visit Hugo. My parents, slightly mollified by my diplomas, had expected me to rush out immediately in search of suitable employment, and their quite genuine pleasure in welcoming me home had worn noticeably thin as we continued to fall over each other in the tiny Oxford flat.

'Have you been to the island before?' my new friend enquired when I had parried her last question.

I hesitated. 'Apparently not.'

She raised her eyebrows with a laugh. 'Apparently?'

'My family tell me I haven't, but when my brother's appointment came through—he's a master at St Olaf's—I was sure I knew the island. Perhaps I saw a documentary on it once.'

I was looking forward to seeing Hugo again, even though I must now share him with a wife. He had married during my stay in Paris and the only time I'd met Martha was when I'd flown over for the wedding. It had not taken me long to realize that my new sister-in-law was as brilliant as the rest of my family. I could only hope that her presence wouldn't lesssen the rapport which, despite the six-year age gap, had always existed between Hugo and me.

The long descent had already begun and I turned to look out of the window, eager not to miss my first glimpse of the island.

'That's Douglas down there,' my companion informed me. 'Doesn't it look grand with the lights all round the bay?'

The rushing landscape beneath us was coming closer and closer and minutes later we touched down at Ronaldsway Airport. People were already on their feet and further up the aisle the man I had thought I knew was taking his briefcase from the rack.

'Have a nice holiday, dear!'

I said good-bye to my travelling companion and when I looked back he had gone. With a small sigh I freed myself from the seat-belt and collected my things.

Hugo was waiting in the airport buildings, huge and welcoming and more bear-like than ever with the addition of a new beard.

'Chloe! *Comment ça va?* Good to see you!'

I returned his hug with enthusiasm. 'Good to see you, too! It's been a long time.'

'I left Martha at home struggling with dinner. I'd better warn you that cookery just isn't her scene. Poor lamb, she's terrified at the prospect of entertaining a Cordon Bleu professional!'

'She's frightened of me? I don't believe it! I'm the one with the inferiority complex! You know how I retreat into my shell at the first hint of intellectual conversation!'

He laughed. 'I can see I'm going to have a great time running from one of you to the other with words of encouragement! Here's the luggage coming now. Which is yours?'

I pointed out my case, Hugo retrieved it and I followed him out through the windy darkness to the parked car.

'I'm afraid you won't see much tonight.'

'It's strange, but I still have this feeling I've been here before. There's a clear picture in my mind of glens and round-topped hills.'

'Which description, though accurate, doubtless fits quite a few places! By the way, you realize you're no longer in the United Kingdom?'

'Really? How's that?'

'I'll leave Martha to explain. She's become quite absorbed in the island's history—even thinking of doing a paper on it.'

'I thought art was her subject?'

'She read history as well. That's how we met.'

'Clever girl! Didn't you say in a letter that she teaches at St Olaf's too?'

'Part-time, yes. She takes art classes three afternoons a week. We're only ten minutes' drive from college so it's quite convenient. We could have lived in Staff House, of course, but we'd had enough of communal life at varsity. There's something very satisfactory about being able to retreat behind your own front door at the end of the day.'

'Do the rest of the staff live in?'

'Some. Quite a few of the married members have flats in Mona Lodge, just outside Ballacarrick.'

'And your cottage is actually in the village?'

'Yes, but Manx villages aren't like English ones. No neat little village green with a duck pond and general stores. Most of them simply consist of a straggle of houses with a church and school alongside. This is St John's we're skirting now, where Tynwald is held every summer. You've heard of it, I suppose, the island's independent parliament?'

I rubbed a circle in the steam on the car window, but the rain sluicing down outside proved an impenetrable barrier. 'I think so. Does the world Tynwald mean "parliament"?'

'Yes, and it's also used for the actual ceremony held once a year. It comes from "thing"—assembly, and "vollr" field. The legislative system is Scandinavian, of course, and the whole place is steeped in history. Perhaps that's why it appeals to us so much!'

Something in his words touched a chord inside me and set it vibrating. Everyone was so sure I had never been here, and yet—

'I hope the weather holds for you,' Hugo was continuing. 'This rain should have cleared by morning but if the mist comes down you won't be able to do much.'

Mist. Again, more strongly, some inner

7

memory stirred. The word seemed to materialize, cloaking itself in its own trailing shroud and wrapping round me with a deep, penetrating chill. Mist, the forlorn cry of seabirds—and a feeling of sudden, unexplained terror. I shivered involuntarily.

'Cold? This heater's on the blink, I'm afraid. Not much further, though.'

The car sped on under writhing, wind-torn trees, between thickly wooded plantations, past isolated cottages crouching in the shadows. My heart began to flutter uncomfortably at the base of my throat. Steeped in history, Hugo had said. And folklore too, I felt certain. No race could have lived here all these centuries without becoming aware of other, unseen inhabitants, timeless as the hills themselves.

'Home stretch!' Hugo's voice made me jump. 'That was Ballaugh we've just come through. We'll be there in a couple of minutes now. Here's the turning.' We left the main road and a moment later swung into a driveway and the car came to a halt, its wheels churning gravel. To our left a porch light shone in welcome. Hugo took my arm and ran with me through the driving rain to the shelter of the cottage where Martha was waiting to greet us. She was a tall girl, only an inch or so shorter than Hugo, with long dark hair and helpless-looking eyes behind enormous horn-rimmed spectacles.

'Hello, Chloe. Welcome to the Isle of Man!'

She turned to Hugo who kissed her soundly and for a brief moment I felt an outsider. Then his other arm came round my shoulders. 'Chloe's a bit chilly. Is there a good fire going?'

I followed Martha through the door on the right into a fair-sized room dominated by a stone fireplace where an open fire crackled cheerfully. Thick woven curtains in warm orange shut out the wind-filled night. There were deep, patently comfortable armchairs, a sofa, shelves and shelves of books, and Hugo's old desk in one corner. Immediately at home, I moved to the hearth and held out my hands.

'How lovely to see an open fire after years of central heating and smokeless zones!'

Hugo selected a log from the side of the hearth and threw it on the fire. 'Sit down and warm yourself. I'll put the case in your room.'

Left alone, Martha and I smiled at each other a little nervously and both started to speak at the same time. I said: 'I hear you teach at St Olaf's.' And she: 'I hope Hugo warned you to bring indigestion tablets!'

We laughed and the ice was broken.

'How was France?' she asked eagerly. 'I'm longing to hear about it.'

'Hard work most of the time. We didn't get much chance to socialize.'

'What a waste! Didn't you meet any devastating Frenchmen?'

'There was one, at the hotel where I worked

9

during the summer. I've had a couple of letters since I came back.' Fleetingly I thought of Jean-Claude and the warm, Mediterranean nights. It seemed—it was—another world from this dark, wet little island in the middle of the Irish Sea.

'I do hope you'll make allowances for my cooking,' Martha was saying anxiously. 'As Hugo probably told you, I flap around in an aura of burned pans and hard potatoes. He has lunch at college during the week, which has saved him from an ulcer so far, and luckily there's a good little restaurant quite near where we go if my attempt at dinner is a complete write-off.'

That she wasn't exaggerating was unfortunately soon apparent. The delicious-smelling casserole proved to be undercooked, the carrots hard and the meat stringy. Hugo and I chewed on stoically while Martha, almost in tears, kept up a stream of apology. Only when the plates had been cleared away and cheese and biscuits produced were we able to teeter back on to an even conversational keel.

'Any thoughts on the future, Chloe?' Hugo asked, handing me a cup of coffee. 'How are you planning to make use of that impressive array of diplomas?'

'At the moment I haven't a clue.' But his casual enquiry was having the opposite effect from my parents' pointed questioning and already the first tentative ideas were beginning

10

to take shape in my head. 'I'd really like my own restaurant, but that's aiming rather high at this stage. Perhaps I might start as a freelance chef, advertising my service for dinner parties and so on. There'd be no overheads and the pay should be good. I suppose London would offer the best scope.'

'Imagine cooking because you enjoy it!' Martha said wonderingly.

'It's the only thing I can do. Hugo must have told you I've no brains.'

'I certainly did not, nor is it true. Your talents are non-academic, that's all.'

'Tactfully put!' I set down my coffee cup. 'I'm also quite a good non-academic washer-up, so—'

Martha shook her head. 'Not tonight, Chloe. We can manage perfectly well and you must be tired.'

'If you're sure then, perhaps you'll excuse me. I'd like to do my unpacking, such as it is.'

When everything was put away and I was ready for bed, I drew back the curtains and stood looking out of the window. The wind had blown the rain clouds away and the night was fine and clear. A host of scudding cloudlets sailed quickly over the face of the moon and were gone.

Below me lay the neat little garden and beyond that what appeared to be a field, but the moon wasn't bright enough to show it clearly. A car passed along the road with a brief flare of headlamps. I could only guess that the dark mass which shut off the night sky to my right was one of the island's many hills.

Today, I reflected, had held its share of riddles. My thoughts went back to the tall, fair man who had seemed so much a part of me, though common sense forced me to admit we had never met. And there was the same inexplicable sense of familiarity about this island which I had never visited before.

'Well, here I am,' I said silently to whatever or whomever might be listening. 'What do you want of me?' Then, before any answer could come, I pulled the curtains back across the window and climbed hurriedly into bed. It was not a comfortable question to leave hanging on the night air, and ridiculously I wished I could retract it. The answer might be more than I was prepared to accept.

CHAPTER TWO

That night I had one of the 'special' dreams which I had come to anticipate with an equal mixture of curiosity and dread. There was no easy definition of them, for apart from their brilliant clarity they had no uniformity. Some were long and involved and some over as soon as I registered them, a single blazing picture branded on my brain; but whatever their length or content I woke from them keyed to an unnatural pitch of excitement which lasted throughout the following day.

The dream my first night on the island belonged to the distant past, and holding my mind passive I went through the now-established routine of 'playing it back'. The strongest remaining impression was of heat, a golden summer day with the sun directly overhead, its fierce glare glancing off the helmets and shields with an intensity which hurt the eyes. In the foreground a small oddly shaped hillock was peopled with important-looking men and on the topmost tier a man in rich robes sat under a canopy listening to a charge read in some language I couldn't understand.

And that was all; just the memory of sun blazing from a molten sky and the subdued excitement of a vast crowd milling round the foot of the mound.

The sound of running bath water filtered into my consciousness and I filed away the dream in the mental slot prepared for it and turned to more immediate matters. It was Sunday morning, my first day on the island. I swung my feet out of bed and went to the window. The rain had vanished, the wind dropped and the view before me was breathtaking.

Beyond the shining pathway of the garden and its tangle of dew-wet flowers lay a hedge of bright yellow gorse gleaming in the morning sunshine, while to the right the solid blackness of last night revealed itself as a hillside richly covered with multicoloured trees, a hundred varieties of gold and brown and different shades of green. In a corner of the field beyond the garden crouched another whitewashed bungalow and a plume of blue smoke was curling its tentative way into the clear air.

There was a tap on the door and Martha, swathed in a quilted housecoat, put her head round it. 'I heard you draw back the curtains. Like a cup of tea?'

'I'd love one.' I slipped on my dressing-gown and followed her to the kitchen. 'What a fabulous view! You must have painted it countless times!'

'But never to my satisfaction. Landscape isn't my strong suit, anyway.'

'What do you teach?'

'Life mostly. My colleague covers the rest of the field. He's incredibly good, not only as an artist but in the way he can put it over, though it hurts me to say so!'

'You don't like him?'

'Can't stand him—no-one can! But don't let's waste time talking about him. We were wondering if you'd like to come to the little local church this morning? We alternate between it and the college chapel. It's only about two hundred years old, but there are

14

foundations of at least three ancient keeils in the graveyard, not to mention one of the famous Manx crosses which dates from about the sixth century.'

Hugo had wandered in, his hair curling from the steam in the bathroom. 'Martha tends to forget that the facts she's dug up aren't all common knowledge,' he remarked, sitting down beside me. 'If, as I suspect, you've never heard of the "famous Manx crosses", don't be afraid to say so.'

'Then I haven't, nor of a—keeil, did you say? What's that?'

Martha refilled my cup. 'A primitive Celtic church built by Irish missionaries in the fifth century or so. They were very small and usually had a tiny circular cell alongside for the priest. If you're interested I can show you a good example at Lag-ny-Killey—'

'Oh darling, hang on! Not before breakfast!'

She flushed and laughed. 'Sorry, I do tend to get carried away!'

'I'd love to see your keeil, Martha,' I said staunchly. 'In fact, I hope to explore the whole island while I'm here. How big is it?'

'Roughly thirty miles by eleven, I think, at the widest point. Not large, but there's plenty to see: prehistoric burial grounds, standing stones, hill forts, runic crosses—you name it, we've got it! Our idea of a perfect weekend is to set out with a picnic lunch and wander wherever the mood takes us. Then we spend the evening checking what we've seen against Martha's reference books.'

Hugo cooked the breakfast that morning, mounds of crisply fried bacon, mushrooms from the adjoining field and farm eggs. I who had existed in France on *café filtre* and the occasional *brioche* ate hungrily and enjoyed every mouthful. In the end we had to hurry to be in time for church.

St Stephen's was as interesting as Martha had promised. The walls were of slightly porous Manx stone and there was a gentle air of decay about the worn, almost illegible epitaphs of long-dead Manxmen. The little congregation sang lustily, the curate preached an interesting sermon, and afterwards, back in the warming sunshine, Martha led me round to inspect the Manx cross.

'It depicts the legend of Sigurd and the dragon Fafni,' she explained. 'There are several crosses dotted round the island with different scenes from the legend so that taken together they form a kind of stone story book. Admittedly the figures aren't easy to decipher, but this is supposed to be Sigurd's horse Grani—see?—and if you look carefully you can just make out the scales of the dragon down in that corner.'

'It's—incredible,' I said. I had a curious sensation of being drawn forward into the heart of the stone, and far from having difficulty in making out the representations carved on it, the details filled themselves in for me to such an extent that I could almost see the sweat on Grani's flanks and the blood spurting from the heart of the dragon. 'Isn't that—a dwarf—down there on the left?' I murmured hesitantly. I had only just bitten back the name 'Regin' and waited, scarcely breathing, for Martha to confirm it.

She bent forward excitedly, peering through her spectacles. 'Do you know, I believe you're right! However did you distinguish that? It must be Regin, waiting for the chance to betray Sigurd.'

The stone blurred alarmingly and I put out a hand to steady myself, grateful for the reassuring grasp of Hugo's hand. 'All right, Chloe?'

'Yes. Yes, thanks.' I wanted to run away but my legs wouldn't have supported me, to escape from my uncanny knowledge of the ancient Norse legend which, as we turned to walk from the churchyard, Martha was painstakingly relating to me. And I knew it, I thought numbly, I knew it all. I who at breakfast this morning had admitted my ignorance of the very existence of Manx crosses had become in the space of a drawn breath an expert on at least one of them.

The road down the hill was narrow and winding and it was necessary for Hugo to walk ahead of us. Beside me Martha's voice rattled on, about the Jurby cross which showed Sigurd slaying the dragon, the Malew one of him roasting its heart, and that at Andreas, on which Gunnar was being bitten to death in the snakepit. And the names of Jurby and Malew and Andreas, which surely I had never heard before, were not only familiar to me but conjured up an awareness of their individual locations.

We turned off the road at last into the lane leading to the cottage and the strangeness that had held me began to ebb away. Later, I resolved, I would tell Hugo and Martha about it, but first I needed to come to terms with it myself. I was not yet prepared to risk another breath-freezing plunge into the dark folklore of Scandinavia, and throughout lunch I chatted determinedly about my months in France.

'I'm delighted it turned out so well,' Hugo remarked complacently. 'So when you leave here you're off to try your luck in the Big City? Hard on the parents; they've scarcely seen you during the last two years.'

'I don't think they'll shed any tears,' I replied lightly, and, at his raised eyebrows, went on quickly, 'Oh Hugo, you know as well as I do that I'm an embarrassment to them! Once they realized I wasn't going to amount to anything they opted out. Or rather,' I corrected myself with a small laugh, 'they simply didn't opt in! They'd no interest in us as young children,' I explained to Martha. 'Esmé escaped at the earliest opportunity and left us to a string of nannies. I always felt I missed out on something and built up a positive barrage of inhibitions. It didn't affect Hugo, though. He slipped neatly into gear and fulfilled all their expectations and they were able to sit back complacently and applaud from the sidelines.'

Hugo said quietly, 'I appreciate they were hardly doting parents, but I'd no idea you felt so strongly about it. Is that why you went to France?'

'Partly. Esmé obviously took my lack of achievement as a personal insult and I had the distinct impression that I was bad for business!' I glanced at him, noting his frown. 'Don't look so worried, brother dear, I'm used to it now. All I was trying to say was that if I go to London there will be nothing but relief all round. I'm welcome at Oxford as a visitor, but that's all.'

Martha put her hand over mine. 'You're welcome here, anyway, for as long as you'd like to stay.'

'That's sweet of you. Tell you what: you show me round the island and in return—if you'd like me to—I'll give you some tips on cooking.'

'Will you?' Martha's face lit up. 'It's a deal!' She turned to Hugo. 'Beloved, all is not lost!'

'Unfortunately,' he answered with a smile, 'cooking requires a certain amount of concentration, and if your head is stuffed full of ship burials or you're worrying about the light fading before you've finished your canvas, the odds are you'll still end up with disintegrated potatoes, however well Chloe instructs you!'

'See the faith he has in me!' Martha said ruefully. 'Still, I'm an eternal optimist and if I can just watch you preparing meals—if you wouldn't mind, that is—I'm sure I'll learn a lot.'

Hugo threw back his head and laughed. 'Chloe, my sweet, that is my wife's way of informing you that you may take over the cuisine for as long as you're here!'

'Oh—I didn't mean—' Martha stammered.

'But I wouldn't mind, honestly. In fact it would ease my conscience over perhaps stretching my visit from one week to two, if that would be all right?'

'You heard what Martha said. We'll be delighted to have you for as long as you want to stay.'

After the meal, Hugo went out to the garden and Martha and I cleared the table. I was wondering with a touch of bewilderment why, entirely without previous thought, I had asked to extend my visit. In view of my experience in St Stephen's churchyard the more sensible course would surely have been to curtail it.

It was as Martha dried the last plate and I

was rinsing round the bowl that she exclaimed suddenly, 'Oh no! Not that!'

'What is it?' I straightened and followed her glance out of the window. A man was leaning on the gate talking to Hugo, and once again the safe, warm present fragmented like a shaken kaleidoscope and reformed to show a symbolic black cloud hanging over the stranger's head. As I blinked incredulously he turned towards the house and in the same instant a needling pain zigzagged like a current through my head. I caught my breath as Martha said disgustedly, 'That's all we need! The surest way to ruin a Sunday afternoon!'

'Who is it?' I asked carefully.

'Ray Kittering, the art master I was telling you about. Oh blast! Hugo's sure to ask him in for a cup of tea.'

'Why don't you like him?' I was conscious of a curious empathy with the dark-haired man at the gate, a feeling as totally without reason as my cognizance in the churchyard earlier.

'It would take too long to go into,' Martha answered curtly. 'There! What did I tell you?' Presumably at Hugo's invitation, Ray Kittering had pushed open the gate and they were both walking towards the house. Martha opened the back door. 'Hello, Ray. We saw you from the window.'

'Good afternoon.' His eyes, large and dark, moved to me and the odd little current, less painful this time, shot through me again. I couldn't put a name to it; it was nothing as commonplace as physical attraction.

'Chloe, this is Ray Kittering from St Olaf's,' Hugo was saying. 'My sister, Ray.'

He held out his hand and, still confused by my reactions, I took it rather hesitantly. 'I hear this is your first visit? I'd be glad to show you round the island some time.' His voice was soft, with an Irish intonation offset against a hint of the north country. I found it curiously attractive. Hugo took him through to the sitting-room and Martha said quietly, 'I shouldn't fall for that line. You don't want to be tied to the like of him while you're here.'

'Surely he's not that bad?' I said defensively. 'I got the impression he's rather unsure of himself.'

She regarded me with open amazement. 'Whatever gave you that idea? He's about as unsure of himself as a boa constrictor!'

I flashed a curious glance at our guest as I carried through the tray. There was nothing in his appearance to excite such antipathy. He was slightly built, of medium height, with dark hair shaggy over his ears, a thin nose and a mouth that looked as though it could be petulant. Without doubt his eyes were his best feature, dark and slumbrous with thick sweeping lashes.

'One without milk,' I said quickly as Martha started to pour.

'Thanks, I was forgetting.' She looked up.

22

'For Ray, you mean? How did you know that?'

I stared back at her, pulses suddenly racing, aware that I was the focus of everyone's interested attention. 'I've—no idea!' I faltered.

'I was just about to remind her myself,' Ray said slowly. 'Have you the sight, Chloe Winter, or was it the little people whispering in your ear?'

With a smilingly incoherent disclaimer I handed him his tea but his eyes followed me as I moved away and sat down.

'Well, I've a touch of it myself, and there's something I know for sure. You'll be over here for a long time yet, I'd take a bet on it.'

'Then I'm afraid you'd lose it,' I said breathlessly. 'I'm only on holiday, two weeks at the most.'

He shook his head decidedly. 'I feel it in my bones and I'm never mistaken. You belong here, somehow. You should have come years ago.'

Catching Martha's frown I hastily picked up my teacup. Hugo was saying something about St Olaf's but I scarcely heard him. Of their own volition my eyes returned to Ray Kittering and encountered his steady gaze. A strange excitement began to flow over me, and the physical attraction I'd discounted suddenly asserted itself, drying my mouth and setting my heart pounding. Dimly I was aware that our concentration on each other was causing Hugo

23

and Martha some embarrassment but I was as powerless to break away as a hypnotized rabbit. And as the phrase came into my mind a nerve jerked agonizingly and at last I was able to drop my eyes.

Immediately Ray broke into the conversation. 'When can I see you?' It was blunt to the point of rudeness, completely excluding the others in the room.

'I don't know.'

His excitement, only partly physical, was coming across in great scarlet waves of emotion. 'Tonight?'

'I'm sorry,' Hugo put in smoothly, making a stand at last. 'We have other plans for this evening.'

'I'll phone you, then.' Ignoring Hugo, he spoke directly to me but Martha, roused by Hugo's intervention, came to his assistance.

'To what do we owe the pleasure of this visit anyway?' she asked acidly.

His concentrated attention shifted at last and I felt myself go limp, as though strings which had been manipulating me had suddenly slackened.

'You asked for the set of folios I'd collected. I put them on the hall table.'

'Thank you.'

There was a brief, splintered silence and Ray, finally interpreting the atmosphere in the room, rose to his feet. Without a word Martha preceded him to the door and held it open.

'I'll be in touch,' he said, and was gone. Hugo, with an expressive glance at his wife, followed him.

'What happened, Chloe?' Martha was regarding me with a puzzled frown. 'You just seemed to—go under.'

That was it, exactly. Under—submerged—incapable of thought or breath. 'He's very attractive,' I said unsteadily.

'So I've been told, though I can't see it myself. Everyone at college loathes him. You asked me why earlier. For one thing, he goes out of his way to upset people, but it's more than that. Sometimes in the Common Room he sits watching me, smiling slightly, and I get the creepy feeling that he knows exactly what I'm thinking.' She shuddered. 'Not to put too fine a point on it, he *frightens* me. I know it sounds crazy, but there it is.'

Hugo came back into the room. 'Well, he certainly gave you the full treatment, didn't he? I've never seen him in action before. Take my advice and give him a wide berth, my girl. You're supposed to be here to enjoy yourself and I don't want to have to pick up any broken pieces.'

'Why couldn't I see him tonight?'

Hugo eyed me speculatively. 'Because we're going out for drinks.'

'Are we?' Martha looked surprised.

'As of now, yes. A few of the crowd congregate at the King Orry on Sunday

25

evenings. There's no reason why on this occasion we shouldn't join them.'

'In other words it was just an excuse.' I stared at him sullenly, resenting his intervention.

'It was,' he confirmed blandly, 'and a much needed one, I felt.'

'To protect me from Ray Kittering?' My voice was heavy with sarcasm.

'To protect you from yourself,' Hugo answered sombrely. 'Now stop being awkward, there's a good girl. I've no intention of standing by while Ray devours you, so you might as well accept the fact.'

I regained my equilibrium during the afternoon and after a light supper we duly set out for the King Orry, an attractive little inn outside Ballaugh. The oak-beamed room, dominated by a brass-canopied chimney-piece, was filled to capacity. Hugo guided Martha and myself over to the far corner, where a group of people were talking animatedly. They turned to welcome us and the blood suddenly rushed to my face in a wave of excitement. Two feet away from me was the man I had so nearly run to greet in the departure lounge at Heathrow.

Hugo, totally oblivious of my confusion, introduced him in turn. 'Neil Sheppard, my sister Chloe.'

He held out his hand. 'Didn't we come over on the same plane yesterday?'

'Yes, I believe so.' It was as useless to pretend I didn't remember him as to deny the deep sense of familiarity which once more flooded over me. Even his voice was well known to me, and the way his mouth lifted slightly at one corner when he smiled—

Mechanically I responded to the other names Hugo was reeling off—Pam Beecham, Martin and Sheila Shoesmith, John Stevens, Simon and Carol Fenton.

'Are you over here for long?' Neil asked, handing me a glass. I felt Pam Beecham glance at me quickly.

'About two weeks, I think. I haven't seen Hugo and Martha for some time.'

'You were wise to wait till the season was over. Provided the weather holds, the island is at its best at this time of the year. Didn't Hugo say you've been in France?'

'Yes, for almost two years.'

'Doing cookery, wasn't it?' put in Carol Fenton. 'We'll have to persuade you to pass on a few tips while you're here!'

'Will you be going back to France?' Pam enquired.

'I don't think so, but I haven't any definite plans yet.' Jean-Claude wanted me to return for Christmas. If I did, I knew it would be taken as a sign that our interest in each other was serious.

'Neil, I meant to tell you:' Pam tucked her arm possessively in his. 'I was able to get an

27

extra ticket after all, if you'd like to come.'

'Ticket?'

'For the concert at Port Erin.'

'Oh yes. Thanks.'

Talk became more general and I didn't have a chance to speak to Neil again. On the way home in the car I said casually, 'Is Neil Sheppard at St Olaf's too?'

'Yes, they all are. I like Neil; he's been a good friend to us since we came.'

'When I saw him at the airport yesterday I was sure we'd met before.'

'It's unlikely. He's been here about six years and his people live in Hertfordshire.'

'Pam seems to be stepping up the attack!' Martha remarked with a giggle.

'So I noticed, but I doubt if she'll make much progress. Neil's not one to be stampeded.' Hugo's eyes met mine in the driving mirror. 'Enjoy your evening after all, Chloe?'

'Yes, thank you.' With a sense of almost guilty surprise I realized that since meeting Neil I had entirely forgotten Ray Kittering. Two hours earlier I should not have believed that possible.

It had been an eventful day. Perhaps the stimulation of last night's dream had made me receptive both to the legend of the cross and later to Ray. But what of my 'recognition' of Neil? Instead of lessening as might have been expected on closer acquaintance, it had deepened still further and I was no nearer being able to explain it.

I fell asleep with thoughts of Ray, Neil and St Stephen's jostling for prominence in my mind—and woke, I don't know how much later, to find Hugo standing over me shaking my arm.

'What is it? What's happened?' I stared up at him uncomprehendingly.

'I was about to ask you the same thing. You were shouting and screaming fit to waken the dead!'

'I was?' Behind him in the lighted doorway Martha was hovering anxiously.

'Yes, a frightful commotion. You must have been dreaming.'

'I'm sorry I disturbed you,' I said after a moment.

'It doesn't matter since you're all right, but it was quite a performance. A load of foreign-sounding gibberish. Fair gave me the willies!' added my scholastic brother. He looked down at me a moment longer. 'Sure you're all right?'

'Quite, thank you.'

'O.K. See you in the morning, then.' With his hand under Martha's elbow he pulled the door shut behind him.

And it was then, without warning, that the 'voice' slid into my mind, bringing as always a shaft of pure fear. This phenomenon had first happened several years ago at much the same time as the dreams started, but while I'd recounted those until my parents' obvious lack of interest discouraged me, this other strangeness I'd kept fearfully to myself. Those who heard voices were after all distinctly suspect. Not that it was a voice as such. It filtered directly into my understanding without sound or visual image, compelling, personal and anonymous, and its message was always the same. *'Come to me! I'm waiting for you.'*

At first I'd tried to signal back: *'Who are you? What do you want?'* but there was never any reply. It seemed I was equipped to receive but not transmit.

Yet that night after Hugo had left me there was for the first time a difference. It was nearer and clearer than ever before and excited exultation replaced the usual longing.

'You recognized me! Why did you take so long to come?'

And as, without hope, I tried once again to establish contact, it switched off and my mind was my own again.

You recognized me. Tumultuous conjectures went clattering round my head and would not be silenced. Neil? Ray? Or one of the others who had been at the King Orry the previous evening? And was it then to the Isle of Man that the 'voice' had been summoning me over the past five years? If so, now that I was here, what would happen?

On a wave of escalating fear my mind suddenly went blank and, dreamlessly, I slept.

CHAPTER THREE

Hugo and Martha were at the breakfast table when I reached the kitchen the next morning.

'Sorry to have started without you, but I have to leave in a few minutes and it seemed a pity to wake you, especially after your disturbed night.' He looked up at me with narrowed eyes. 'How are you this morning?'

'Fine,' I answered firmly, sliding into my chair and accepting a cup of tea from Martha.

'No after-effects of your nightmare?'

'None. I don't remember dreaming at all.' Which was true. Not dreaming—

'It wasn't one of your glorious Technicolor extravaganzas, then?'

I flashed him a quick look and went on stirring my tea. 'No.'

'Her what?' Martha demanded.

'She went through a phase some years ago of extraordinarily vivid dreams. Do you still have them, Chloe?'

There was no point in denial. Dreams, after all, were acceptable, something that happened to everyone. 'From time to time.'

'How do they differ from ordinary dreams?' Martha asked with interest.

'They're so real. When I think about them afterwards, it's like remembering things I've actually done. Sometimes I'm not even sure

31

whether they happened or not.'

'Have you always had dreams like that?'

'No, only the last few years.'

'Which is odd,' Hugo commented, folding his table napkin. 'Something must have triggered them off. When exactly did they start—can you pinpoint it?'

That was something I'd carefully tried to avoid. 'Four or five years ago, I suppose,' I answered evasively.

He looked up sharply. 'Since that business with the hypnotist?'

'Probably, yes.'

'What hypnotist? Hugo, what is all this?'

He bent to kiss her. 'I'll have to leave Chloe to tell you or I'll be late for prayers. See you in the staff-room about three.' He flashed me a smile. 'Have a good day, little sister.'

Martha didn't even turn her head. 'Chloe? Do explain!'

My skin was tingling, as though the suspicion—almost the certainty—which I had been suppressing for so long was bubbling to the surface in a series of small electric explosions.

I said tonelessly, 'I had rather an unpleasant experience when I was sixteen. A crowd of us went to a variety show where there was one of those mind-reader-cum-hypnotist acts and I volunteered to go up on the stage.'

'More than I'd have done! Was he able to put you under?'

'Oh yes,' I answered grimly, 'there was no problem about that. What he couldn't do was bring me round again.'

Martha's eyes were like saucers behind her glasses. 'Whatever happened?'

'They rushed me to hospital and I was out for about three days.'

'And you don't remember anything about it?'

'Not a thing.'

'How ghastly! It ought to be illegal, doing that kind of thing for entertainment.'

'It isn't, though. The parents tried to file a claim for personal injuries, but it wouldn't hold up because I'd volunteered to take part.'

'And you reckon the dreams might date from then? I shouldn't be at all surprised! What are they actually about?'

'They vary. Some seem to be set in the past—you know, swords and things, while others are obviously modern.'

'And I suppose since they seem so real the background and everything must be appropriate to the occasion, not way-out as in ordinary dreams.'

I looked across at her. 'You know, that's strange; it hadn't struck me before, but now that you mention it the backgrounds are always much the same, hills and moorland and the sea. Which is also strange, because I've never spent any time near the sea in my life. Even in the south of France I was up in the mountains.'

'Well, you're certainly surrounded by it now.'

'Yes.' I buttered my toast thoughtfully. 'Sometimes I seem to be searching for someone. I've dreamed that several times.'

'It sounds fascinating. I wish I had interesting dreams. Mine are all the usual jumble like finding I'm walking into college in my nightdress. Hugo says it shows a basic lack of confidence.'

'I have my share of that kind, too.'

'Talking of walking into college, this is one of my afternoons there. Would you like to come? You could even model for us if you wouldn't mind—circumspectly clothed, of course! The boys get so tired of drawing each other and they never keep still anyway. We could meet Hugo for a cup of tea in the staff-room afterwards.'

'I don't promise to sit for you, but I'd like to see the college. How many boys are there?'

'Two hundred, most of them boarders and nearly all from the mainland. It's smaller than King William's and hasn't been going as long, but it's notching up quite a tradition of its own.' She pushed back her chair. 'Any plans for this morning? I'm afraid I'll have to stay in and see to the washing, but if you'd like to take the car you could drive round a bit and get your bearings.'

I glanced out of the window. Yesterday's

34

sunshine had gone. The morning was clear and grey and a scarf of mist trailed nonchalantly over the hill. 'I'm sure to get lost!'

'The roads are reasonably well sign-posted, but I'll lend you my Ordnance Survey.'

'All right, I'll risk it! What time is your class?'

'Two o'clock. If we eat at one there'll be plenty of time.'

I found that motoring on the island was a thoroughly agreeable experience, with none of the traffic jams of home. In fact all I saw was an occasional farm tractor. I turned off the main road and drove slowly along winding lanes, regretting that the high-banked hedges obscured some of the loveliest views. There seemed to be a thriving reafforestation programme, with plantations of trees spreading a rich cloak over the hillsides. Every now and again the road ran alongside a river which over the centuries had eaten its way through the underlying rock to form deep gorges displaying slabs of shining Manx slate and gradually as I drove the peaceful surroundings soothed away the stresses left by my nightly communication and I relaxed into contented acceptance. Perhaps this lovely little island, unknown to me but half-remembered, was where I was supposed to be. And here at last, spread out before me, lay the sea.

It was a jagged stretch of coastline, with the water whipped into short choppy wavelets continually breaking and creaming against the rocks. I stopped the car at the side of the road and wound down the window. The air was alive with wheeling gulls and the haunting lament of their cries filled the vast spaces of sea and sky. I sat motionless for long minutes, letting the familiarity of it all sink into me. Could any forgotten childhood memory produce such total recognition?

An old man was coming down the road towards me, a sheep-dog at his heels, but even as I watched him approach I was suddenly, inexplicably down on the sand far below surrounded by a throng of people laughing and jostling each other. Dotted along the shore were the remains of driftwood fires and round each one young people were clustering, darting their fingers into the warm grey ashes to retrieve round cakes of barley bread.

Panic sluiced over me. What was happening? Was it a dream? Even the most vivid of them had never been like this. The sand was cold and ridged under my bare feet— bare?—and my nostrils were filled with the smell of charred wood mixed with a strong pungent odour of seaweed. Beside me a broad-shouldered young man was cracking open the shell of a baked limpet in his teeth.

Barley bread? Limpet? No-one was taking any notice of me and now people were stamping out the last sparks in the dying fires and a few couples began to form into a chain, winding over the sand in a curious kind of dance. I turned to the young man beside me, wondering if I was expected to join in—and became joltingly aware of the steering-wheel biting into my clutching fingers. The old man and his dog were just coming abreast of the car. His face creased into a smile and he touched his cap. Somehow I managed to smile and nod in return. Then he had passed and I was alone again.

Fearfully my eyes went to the seashore far below, but all I could see were the waves breaking endlessly over the pointed rocks. What had happened to the strong young man with his bare feet and coarsely textured jacket? Had he and his companions existed only in my imagination, or in some time other than my own? My rapid heartbeats made breathing difficult. It was a dream, I told myself urgently. That was the only possible explanation. I even knew from the old man's approach the exact duration of it. But was it possible to fall so instantly and totally asleep and to waken again all in the space of two or three minutes? Before, my dreams had decently confined themselves to my sleeping hours. The prospect of their emergence into daily existence filled me with unease. And it had been so very real—

Determinedly pushing all the speculations away I leant forward and switched on the ignition.

It was only as I drew up outside the cottage, still dazed and bewildered by my experience, that I remembered my promise to see to the meals during my stay. It was obviously too late. Fiercely bubbling baked beans were sticking to the pan on the stove and a smell of burned toast filled the kitchen.

Martha appeared from the hall, magnificently unpertubed. 'Hello! Where did you get to?'

Over our less than perfect lunch I told her the route I had taken, though I didn't mention the 'dream'. That, like my knowledge of the Sigurd legend, I intended to keep to myself for the moment. 'If I were an artist I'd go mad with frustration!' I remarked lightly. 'Absolutely everything cries out to be painted!'

'It is lovely, specially now the bracken's turned that gorgeous golden brown. Actually, Ray—' She bit her lip and glanced at me guiltily.

'Ray what?'

'I was just going to say he's done some marvellous paintings of the island, in all the different seasons.'

'Then why did you break off?'

She hushed. 'Hugo thinks it would be better if we played Ray down a bit, after yesterday. I suppose I really shouldn't be taking you to college. I hadn't thought of that.'

I said tightly, 'My dear Martha, I don't need a wet-nurse. I'm perfectly capable of taking care of myself without you and Hugo flapping round like distracted hens!'

'Yes, of course. I'm sorry.' She smiled at me rather uncertainly and changed the subject.

My first view of St Olaf's was across a stretch of playing-fields, a collection of grey stone buildings round a central square, set in extensive grounds.

'Impressive, isn't it?' Martha slowed down to enable me to take in the panorama. 'This is the back view but the road follows the boundaries so you'll see it from three sides before we get there. The building jutting out on the right there is the new gym and swimming-pool, and that long low building along the back of the quad is the hall, with the library above it.'

We turned right at the corner, and on this shorter side of the rectangle the grounds were partially hidden by five large stone houses facing on to the road like a row of sentinels.

'These are the boarding-houses—Godred, Sigurd, Lagman and Magnus, and this last one on the corner,' as we again turned right to drive along the front boundary wall, 'is Staff House. Hugo and I were there for a while before we found the cottage. This is the most imposing view of college—the one on the prospectus! There's the chapel just inside the gates. We'll come on Sunday so you can see it properly.'

The driveway led between smoothly

stretching lawns to a towering grey stone archway giving on to the quadrangle. Here Martha turned to the left, following a smaller drive round the corner of the buildings to the staff car-park.

'The art and music wing is this side of the quad so we haven't far to walk.' She reached over to the back seat and retrieved the pile of folios Ray had left the day before. 'Right, off we go.'

The magnificent proportions of the buildings, the marble floors, dignified archways and highly polished staircases reminded me strongly of the Oxford colleges. A group of boys came through the door behind us, speaking in low voices.

'They're on their way back from lunch,' Martha explained. 'There's no dining-hall so they have all their meals in their own houses.'

'Where does Hugo eat?'

'Staff lunch is served in the common room. You have to sign a book if you'll be in for it.'

We had walked together up one of the sweeping staircases and Martha opened a door into a wide, light studio. There was a scrape of chairs as the boys rose to their feet and I was overtaken by a rush of embarrassment as the battery of respectful but definitely assessing eyes switched from Martha to myself.

'This is my sister-in-law,' she told them, moving to the dais at the far end of the room. 'I'm hoping she'll agree to sit for us.' Which in effect neatly ruled out any opportunity for my refusing.

Aided by willing hands Martha arranged a small chair on the platform, draped it artistically with a swathe of rust-coloured velvet, and settled me in position. Then, with an encouraging smile, she handed me a copy of *Manx Life* and moved away to supervise the class. For the next forty minutes I sat like a rock, only my fingers moving from time to time to turn the pages of the magazine but my thoughts, unanchored, roamed free and they were not reassuring. There was the frightening lapse that morning, for which I still couldn't accept any reasonable explanation, and the 'voice' of the night before, with its talk of recognition. And at the end of this lesson we should go to the staff-room and doubtless see both Neil and Ray. Would one of them come forward and identify himself?

'Right, Chloe, that's it, thank you. Come and see yourself as others see you!'

Easing my aching back I stepped down from the dais and followed Martha as she moved along the rows of easels. It was daunting to see so many different versions of my own face, but the artwork was of an impressively high standard and I listened with fascination to Martha's lucid and constructive criticisms. Occasionally by a line or two of her pencil she was able to bring a portrait instantly to life. The bell rang as we reached the last row and

41

she dismissed the class.

'Thank you, Chloe, that was great. I'm sure they appreciated a new model, even if their efforts to portray you weren't entirely complimentary! Now you've earned yourself a cup of tea.'

At the foot of the mahogany staircase Martha opened a door which led outside into the quadrangle. Here mullioned windows looked down on us from every side and in each corner a small staircase led to the floor above. The whole square was dominated by a handsome clock tower whose chimes rang out above our heads as we emerged.

'There's the hall I showed you from the road,' Martha pointed out. 'We have assembly there and concerts and so on. The Derby Library is on the floor above. And this is the staff-room.'

She opened a small brass-studded door and showed me into a pleasant room seemingly full of people. In the centre was a long refectory table, at one end of which a young woman with a tight blonde bun was dispensing tea. Martha slipped an arm encouragingly through mine and led me towards her.

'This is Phyllis Lathom, who teaches chemistry. There are only four women on the staff, so we're very exclusive! Phyl, meet Hugo's sister, Chloe.'

My lightning coverage of the room had informed me that neither Hugo, Neil nor Ray was present, but as we turned from the tea-urn someone called to us from a group near the window. It was Martin Shoesmith, whom I'd met at the King Orry.

'Hello, Chloe! Martha hasn't wasted much time in dragging you here!'

'She wanted a new model for Six B,' I said ruefully.

'I'm sure they appreciated it! You met John and Simon last night, didn't you? May I introduce Philip Davidson?' A tall, dark man smilingly took my hand. 'And this is Richard Lester, who teaches biology, and Duncan Carnforth, the physics wizard.'

I stood sipping my tea and listening to a lot of small talk which meant nothing to me while my eyes scanned the groups of boys continually crossing and recrossing the quad until at last my vigilance was rewarded. Neil came striding purposefully in the direction of the staff-room, a black gown hanging from his shoulders, and the brass-studded door swung open to admit him.

I watched as he collected his tea and exchanged a laughing comment with Miss Lathom. Then he turned from the table and our eyes met. At the same moment, from higher up the room, Pam Beecham's voice called with an undercurrent of command, 'Over here, Neil!'

He hesitated a moment, then, lifting a hand in acknowledgement in her direction, came across to me. 'This is a pleasant surprise. I didn't expect to see you again so soon.'

I smiled and made some conventional reply but I was thinking: 'Yes, I recognized you, but you didn't seem to know me. Or was that part of the plan, to keep me guessing?' His eyes were on my face but whether there was anything in them other than mild interest I could not tell.

He started to say, 'Perhaps one evening—' and broke off as Pam Beecham came across.

'Apparently the mountain must come to Mahomet!' she said tightly.

'I was just having a word with Chloe.'

'So I see.' Her glance in my direction was not friendly. 'What about the concert tomorrow? I'll have to let Leslie know if we need the extra ticket.'

'I'm sorry, Pam, I didn't realize it was tomorrow. I shan't be able to make it.'

'Why not?'

He raised an eyebrow slightly. 'I have a dinner engagement.'

'But Neil, I asked you over a week ago. Surely—'

'From nagging women and all forms of pestilence, Good Lord deliver us!' I knew without turning my head that Ray had joined us. An indefinable ripple swept through the group as though suddenly everyone was on his guard. Pam Beecham's face flamed.

'When I want any comment from you I shall

44

ask for it!' she said furiously.

Ray turned to me, slipping an arm round my shoulders, and I was uncomfortably aware of Neil's surprise. 'Hello, my lovely! What are you doing here?'

Pam, forgetting her anger, said quickly, 'You've already met?' and her eyes went to Neil with a flicker of malice.

Ray ignored her. 'Well, Chloe?' His eyes, only inches away from mine, blazed into them and beneath the banter the current I'd been aware of before pulsated between us. 'I suppose it's too much to hope that you came to see me?'

'Much too much!' Martha cut in crisply. 'She came because I persuaded her to sit for my class.'

'Well done, Martha! An unexpected stroke of genius! I'd thought of that too, but not in a studio. Out on the hills somewhere, with the wind in her hair.'

'Chloe!' Hugo this time, his voice sharply disapproving. I saw Martha bite her lip and avoid his accusing gaze. Firmly he disengaged me from Ray and led me away from the group to where a thin man with receding fair hair and a bony forehead was standing by himself.

'This is Nicholas Quayle, Chloe. He and his wife have kindly invited us for dinner tomorrow evening.'

'How do you do?' The hand he held out was cold and dry and trembled slightly. I looked up

45

into pale eyes protected by thick glasses, saw the tension repeated there, and wondered at it.

'Nicholas is my fellow history master,' enlarged Hugo.

'And a Manxman to boot!' added Ray, strolling up to join us again. 'There aren't all that many of us on the staff so we stick together, don't we, old boy?'

Any less likely pair would have been hard to imagine and to underline my doubt a muscle tightened spasmodically in the hollow-cheeked face above me. In a brief uneasy silence the sudden rasp of Ray's match as he lit a cigarette came unnaturally loud and Nicholas Quayle started violently. Intuitively I recognized the small deliberate cruelty for what it was, though Ray merely said pleasantly, 'Davis Minor tells me he has another detention this evening. How many does that make this term?'

The expression that flickered in Nicholas's light eyes was gone too quickly for me to define, but it sent a prickle of apprehension up my spine. Before I could fumble after an analysis a bell sounded out in the corridor. With a mumbled excuse Nicholas promptly fled.

'I'll see you and Martha to the car,' Hugo said firmly, and as he shepherded me away I heard Ray's light laugh behind us. Out in the quad Hugo turned to his wife. 'Martha, I expressly warned you—'

'I'm sorry, I'd asked her to sit before I

remembered. Anyway, it was you who started it by inviting him into the house yesterday.'

'What else could I do, for heaven's sake? He'd brought something for you, and I could hardly have anticipated his latching on to Chloe the way he did.'

'Will you both stop talking about me as though I wasn't here!' I said shrilly. 'Surprisingly enough, I have a mind of my own even if its I.Q. isn't half yours!'

'Love, I'm sorry.' Hugo put an arm contritely round me. 'He gets everyone's back up and I'd be much happier if you didn't have anything to do with him, that's all. It gave me the most uncomfortable feeling yesterday, seeing you with him. You seemed to—to dwindle into some kind of puppet. It was macabre.'

A puppet: the idea of controlling strings had occurred to me too. We reached the car and Hugo bent down suddenly and kissed my cheek. 'Home you go, little sister, out of harm's way!'

But was I? Would I ever be again? It was all very well for Hugo and Martha to tell me to avoid Ray, I thought as Martha turned the car out of the college gates, but the option was not mine to make. I was convinced that the forces which had engineered our meeting would not be deflected by any action of mine.

CHAPTER FOUR

'Did Hugo tell you we're invited out for dinner tonight?' Martha asked me as we were preparing to go shopping in Ramsey. 'I can't say I'm particularly looking forward to it; the Quayles aren't the easiest of hosts. You met Nicholas yesterday—tall, with a bit of a stoop. Older than the rest of us.'

'I remember. Why don't you want to go?'

'Well, Vivian can be difficult. Nicholas is all right, except that he's a bundle of nerves and poor Hugo sees enough of him as it is. It's rather sad, really. I gather he came over here with the half-promise of being appointed deputy head, but it didn't come off and his wife can't let him forget it. However,' Martha added with a smile, 'she's a first-class cook, I'll say that for her, so for once you'll have something edible that you haven't prepared yourself!'

The sun was shining as we left the house, though heavy clouds were massing to the north.

'How's your paper on the island going?' I asked. 'Don't forget you promised me a guided tour.' Ray's similar offer was probably in both our minds, but neither of us referred to it.

'I'll be glad to. The research is just a hobby really, though I've become quite hooked on it.

I'm concentrating on pre-history, the very early times before the Stanley dynasty. It was the names of the college houses that first roused my interest—Godred, Sigurd, Lagman and Magnus. They were ancient kings of Man.'

'Kings?'

'Yes, the ruler was known as King for centuries. I think it was Thomas Stanley in the fifteen hundreds who decided he preferred to be "a powerful Lord rather than a petty King". That was when the title became Lord of Man, and it still is.'

'When did it pass to the Crown, then?'

'The first three Edwards each held it briefly, alternating with the Scots. Henry IV gave the island to the Stanleys but Elizabeth I intervened when there were no male heirs and she thought it might be seized by France or Spain. After that it went back to the Stanleys for another hundred and fifty years until it reverted to George III and the title Lord of Man has been held by the British monarch ever since.'

We were coming round a bend of the road and a sweep of countryside lay spread before us, purple and gold under the uncertain sky. Quite suddenly it was all dangerously familiar. Surely it had been here that—

'Careful!' I interrupted sharply. 'Watch out for that sheep—'

Automatically Martha's foot went down on the brake and as the car rocketed to a halt, a black ram broke through the hedge bordering the road. Without my warning it would certainly have been under our wheels. With a startled glance at my white face, Martha pulled in to the side of the road and the animal, ears laid back, set off at an ungainly run down the verge.

'You realize you warned me before that sheep had even appeared?'

'I know.' With an effort I unclenched my hands. 'Martha, this has all happened before. Don't ask me when. I recognized the lay-out of the country, even that broken plough over there, and I remembered you having to brake suddenly. I even knew the sheep was black.'

'*Déjà vu?*' she queried after a moment.

'I suppose it must have been.' I shivered suddenly. 'How horrible!'

'Or,' she went on deliberately, 'could you have dreamed it? One of your extra-sensory specials? You say you keep dreaming of the sea, though till now you've never been near it.' She broke off, leaving the implication of her words to sink in.

'Till now.' There was an insistent drumming of blood in my ears. 'You're surely not suggesting some of the dreams could have been of the future?'

She was watching me intently. 'Couldn't they?'

Neil! The word exploded in my brain, and as I fumbled after its relevance it blindingly

50

clarified itself. That was why I had 'recognized' him at the airport; I knew him from previous dreams, dreams which perhaps were now actually going to come true. It was a possibility I had never even remotely contemplated and I recoiled from it with superstitious horror.

Martha said gently, 'It fits, you know. Precognitive dreams are known to be exceptionally vivid, and you said they seem more like personal memories.'

'But how could they be memories of the future? It just isn't possible!'

'Some people think it is. John Dunne, for example, tied it in with his idea of serial time. Apparently your astral consciousness or other self or whatever it is, is released in sleep and can slip either backwards or forwards in time. So you really would have experienced those things, which is why they seemed familiar.'

My frightened eyes went over the sweep of fields and woodlands lit by dramatic stormy sunshine. It was this identical scene striking a mental replica that had 'broken the dream'. At the airport the sight of Neil had had the same effect. And what of my nebulous connection with Ray? Was that too attributable to my wandering psyche?

Martha laid a hand on my arm. 'Don't look so frightened, love. I believe it's quite a common experience.'

'So you think I actually slipped forward into today, to this particular spot on the Sulby road?'

'Perhaps that's what precognition is, not only knowing in advance but experiencing too. You remember you said the dreams all seemed to be set in the same place? It looks as though it's here, doesn't it? They haven't come true before, because in this dimension of time you've only just arrived.'

The thought had already occurred to me. *'Why did you take so long to come?'*

'But why? Why here, of all the places on earth?' At the back of my mind a possible answer, unwanted and unacknowledged, began to form and I clamped down on it at once. Quite suddenly I didn't want any more revelations, and before Martha could reply I said jerkily, 'Still, we can't sit here all day discussing metaphysics! If we don't hurry the shops will have shut for lunch.'

Accepting my abrupt dismissal of the matter, Martha didn't refer to it again. Nor, though I was sure she mentioned it to Hugo when he came home, did he make any comment. In all probability he was waiting for me to raise the subject but I was still playing ostrich, superstitiously afraid that talking about it would somehow solidify a mere conjecture into fact. I was thankful that the dinner party that evening would provide a distraction for all of us.

The Quayles lived in one of the staff flats in Mona Lodge, a large house in its own grounds

52

just outside Ballacarrick. As we turned into the driveway, thick dark trees closed overhead and our headlamps made only a token tunnel of light. I half expected to find a Gothic castle at the end of it, but in fact the house which came into view was plain and uninteresting, four-square Victorian with not so much as a turret to satisfy the aroused imagination.

Vivian Quayle answered our ring. 'I'm so glad to meet you,' she greeted me as Hugo performed the introductions. 'Lord knows, we don't often see a new face round here. Let me take your coats and come and get warm. I've invited Neil to make up the numbers.'

I was aware of a little spurt of gladness as I followed Martha into the large, comfortably furnished room. This time, presumably, there would be neither Pam nor Ray to interrupt our conversation.

Neil and Nicholas turned from the fireplace to greet us. To my highly attuned senses there seemed a slight reservation in Neil's greeting, due, no doubt, to Ray's proprietorial air yesterday. It was strange how each of them seemed to cancel out the other, so that when I was with one I felt drawn to him alone. The bond with Neil I now knew tied in with my dreams, but I could not gauge how deeply, nor if he was also responsible for the voice. Though I must obviously find out, this was not the time to try and I turned my attention to our host.

In his own home, Nicholas seemed slightly more relaxed than when I had last seen him, a quietly courteous man anxious only for the welfare of his guests. Perhaps the enigmatic Ray had been responsible for his previous agitation, playing one of the cat-and-mouse games which Hugo had warned me about.

Vivian came bustling back. 'Now, what's everybody drinking?' I watched her as she moved about the room, straightening a cushion, fractionally altering the position of an ornament. At first glance she had struck me simply as attractive and smartly dressed, but I was now conscious of a nervous energy about her which made relaxing difficult in her company. In this clearer light, I saw too that the pale, finely chiselled face was criss-crossed by a network of fine lines, though at a guess she was no more than forty. She spoke quickly in staccato sentences, giving the impression that she wasn't prepared to wait for a considered reply.

'And what do you think of Ellan Vannin, Chloe?' she asked, handing me a glass and perching like a bird of passage on the tapestry chair beside me.

'The Isle of Man!' Hugo translated, with a smile for my blankness.

'I haven't seen much of it yet but it seems fascinating.'

'To visit, perhaps,' she said crisply. 'Believe me, it palls surprisingly quickly.'

'It depends what you want from it,' Neil put in. 'There's a gentler pace of living, certainly, but I find the local philosophy "There's another boat tomorrow" rather soothing.'

'Well, I'm afraid I don't. I feel buried alive out here. Oh for department stores, art galleries, concerts, a choice of theatre!' She snapped open her cigarette case, offered it round and selected one for herself with fingers that shook slightly, bending her head to the flame which Neil held out for her.

'Lest Chloe should think she has inadvertently landed on a desert island,' Nicholas observed dryly, 'let me assure her that there are theatres, concert halls and art galleries here. There's even a casino, for heaven's sake, if that's your idea of entertainment. And of course the outdoor facilities can't be bettered: fishing, golf, riding, sailing—'

'You're beginning to sound like a holiday brochure, darling,' Vivian remarked tartly. 'Anyway, it's in your blood, we know that. All I'm saying is that it's not my idea of the bright lights, but I'm well aware that I'm stuck with it. We all are,' she added, her eyes flickering over our rather embarrassed faces, 'except Chloe, lucky child, who can fly out on the next plane without a backward glance whenever the mood takes her.' She stood up and smoothed down her skirt. 'If you'll excuse me I'll go and put the finishing touches to the meal.'

'Is there anything we can do to help?' Martha asked.

'You could carry through the first course for me, if you'd be an angel. No, Chloe, you stay here and entertain the gentlemen. Dinner won't be long.'

'How's the Volvo going, Nicholas?' Hugo enquired as the door closed behind them. He turned to me. 'Did I tell you old Nicholas here has the identical model car I have, colour and all? I did a double take the other day in the staff car-park.'

'No problems so far,' Nicholas replied. 'The only criticism I would make—'

As the conversation became technical Neil sat down on the sofa beside me. 'Don't be put off by Vivian's assessment of the island. It's really a very pleasant little place.'

'I feel rather sorry for her,' I said slowly. 'She seems frustrated somehow.'

'Yes, I'm afraid that's the root of it. The tragedy is that it's mainly on Nicholas's behalf, and if she'd only relax he'd be quite happy here.' He tilted the glass in his hand, his eyes on the swirling liquid. 'How long have you known Ray Kittering?'

The unexpected question took me by surprise. 'Ray? Three days, I suppose. Why?'

He looked up. 'But I understood—I gathered in the staff-room that you knew each other?'

'Only because he'd called at the cottage on

Sunday afternoon.'

'That's all it was? I wondered if perhaps he was part of the reason for your visit.'

My emphatic disclaimer was interrupted by Vivian's announcement that dinner was ready, but as we went through to the dining-room I was uncomfortably aware that I might have been less than honest with Neil. If the compulsive voice in my head was Ray's, he could indeed have influenced my coming, though not in the way Neil had meant.

The meal was excellent but although conversation flowed freely on the surface, I was conscious of the tensions just below. Nicholas's fingers were continually crumbling the bread on his side plate and Vivian laughed too often and on too high a note. Several times I caught Neil's eye across the table and I found my own thoughts wandering, trying to probe back into those dreams in which he had figured and wondering if I should really have the opportunity of reliving them.

'You know, of course, that Nicholas has applied for the Downhurst vacancy?' Vivian remarked to Hugo over the dessert. 'I'm sure he must be better qualified than any of the other applicants. Look at the experience he's had: twenty years now in a succession of famous schools. It's really heart-breaking to see someone of his ability stultifying out here. If he hadn't come to St Olaf's he'd have had his own school years ago.'

'My dear, that is your own rather biased opinion,' Nicholas put in with heightened colour.

'Not only mine, I assure you. It was nothing short of scandalous the way you were passed over in favour of Frank Harrison. After all, it was more or less understood—'

She broke off under the force of pleading in his eyes. 'I'm sorry. Please forgive that outburst. I'm afraid we've both been under rather a strain since the interview. Nicholas is right, of course. You don't want to hear all our problems.'

'By the way, Nicholas,' Neil said smoothly, 'I've been meaning to ask if they've roped you in for the end-of-term play this year?' I caught the grateful glance Vivian flashed him as he turned to me. 'Has Hugo told you what a fantastic mimic Nicholas is? And not just of the "You dirty rat" school! No college entertainment is complete without his impersonation of the prime minister!'

With the conversation steered on to safer topics the evening eventually tottered to a close without any more verbal pitfalls.

'What did you think of them?' Hugo asked as we drove home through the winding dark lanes.

'It wasn't a very comfortable evening, was it? You had to be careful what you said.'

'Too true. Thank heaven at least for Neil.' He put his hand briefly on Martha's knee.

'Never get as neurotic as that about me, will you, sweetheart?'

'Not as long as you're head of Eton before you're forty! Will we have to ask them back? I don't think I could stand the strain!'

'If we do we'll certainly put a spot of bromide in the gravy!' Hugo promised with a laugh as we turned once more into the driveway of the cottage.

CHAPTER FIVE

Yet when I put out my light that night, it was not the undertones and nuances of the evening which occupied my mind but Martha's earlier suggestion that my dreams may now start to play themselves back in waking life. For a long time I tossed and turned wondering about the possible elasticity of time, and it was probably this obsessive treadmill which, when at last I fell asleep, laid me open to the merciless attack of the most terrifying dream I had yet had.

I found myself alone on a hillside in the mist and as always, though I couldn't see it, was aware of the nearness of the sea. Out in the greyness a foghorn sounded mournfully. Where was he? Dear God, what had happened? I started to run, but the long skirt wrapped itself round my legs and I stumbled to a halt. Why had he left me alone? I wanted to call his name, but there was now an ominous listening quality about the stillness, an eerie sensation of not being quite alone after all. In this white blindness someone could be within a few feet of me, waiting for a sound to betray my whereabouts. My eyes strained desperately to penetrate the mist and, as I stared, the drifting whiteness over to my right swirled unaccountably in some eddy of air, thinning to disclose the blurred outline of a man. Slowly he turned his head in my direction and a scream welled up in my throat . . .

Drenched in sweat I lay rigid in Hugo's little guest-room. No use, now, telling myself it was only a dream. It was a 'special' dream, after all, and it seemed these might have a way of coming true. What was more I knew instinctively that despite the long skirt this dream did not lie comfortably in a recurring past but ahead of me, in a future which drew nearer with every tick of my bedside clock. Had I been dreaming of events leading up to my own death? Perhaps that was the reason for bringing me to the island.

It was a long time before I was able to unflex my hands, to force my stiff body to relax, and eventually, as dawn was breaking, to sleep.

I woke a second time that Wednesday morning to the sound of Hugo's car leaving for college, and spent the next few hours trying to persuade Martha to ignore my pallor and the dark circles under my eyes.

'I had a bad night, that's all,' I kept assuring her, and though she probably guessed that bad nights were synonymous with dreams, she didn't press me any further.

'I wish I didn't have a class this afternoon,' she said worriedly over lunch. 'I don't like leaving you, but I suppose you don't want to come with me?'

'Not today Martha, but I'm all right, really.'

And to prove the fact to myself I decided to devote my attention to preparing an elaborate meal for dinner, which would leave me no room for morbid imaginings. We had brought a chicken home from Ramsey the previous day and a quick reconnaissance of the store cupboard showed me that, surprisingly, all the basic ingredients of *Ballotine de Poularde* were to hand. Feeling better already, I tied an apron round my waist and embarked on the delicate task of boning the chicken without cutting through the skin.

I'm not sure at what stage I realized Ray was coming. At first I tried to dismiss my quickened breathing and the unaccountable heat of my body, but when the tap came on the kitchen window and I looked up to see him standing there, it was certainly no surprise. Wiping my hands on the apron I went to let him in.

'Good day to you, Miss Winter.'

'Hello, Ray.' I stood passive, accepting because I had no choice the powerful waves which pulsated over me. After a moment I said with an effort, 'Would you like to come in?'

He smiled slightly. 'Indeed I would. There's not much to be gained from standing on your doorstep! It's a cup of tea I'm after,' he added, following me inside. 'I've a free period and it occurred to me you'd brew a better pot than Phyllis Lathom. It wouldn't surprise me if she concocted hers in the chemistry lab!'

His manner was natural and friendly and could not account for the panic that was beginning to build up inside me. Soon, because I could not help myself, I would have to go to him.

'I'll put the kettle on,' I said carefully, rinsing my hands at the sink. I could feel his eyes on me and the hair on my scalp moved in an age-old reaction to fear. He had stopped talking and in my agitation I could think of no way to break the mounting silence. I took out the cups and saucers which clattered together in my shaking hands and poured the boiling water into the teapot and all the time, as I moved about the room, his eyes followed me. When at last he did speak I actually jumped.

'I phoned you last night. There was no reply.'

'We went to the Quayles for dinner.'

'Then you've my sympathy. If ever a couple were guaranteed to put the dampers on an evening, it's themselves. And was Neil Sheppard there as usual?'

'He was.'

'As I thought. Old Vivian has quite a hankering for him. Might well be mutual, for all she's older than he is. There's more to her than that mewling Pam Beecham, and from her angle wouldn't any man be an improvement on her scared rabbit of a husband, and him preferring little boys anyway.'

I gasped. 'Ray, you can't go round saying things like that! If anyone heard you—'

'What would they do, now? Nothing, I'm telling you. They daren't. There's not one of them hasn't some nasty little secret he'd rather keep hidden.' He glanced at my closed face. 'But I didn't come here to talk about the Quayles, nor, to be truthful, for a cup of tea. You know why I came, don't you, Chloe?'

I shook my head speechlessly.

'You know I can't keep away from you, any more than you can from me.'

A pulse was beating in my throat and my hands were ice cold. This was the moment I'd longed for on Sunday afternoon, when Hugo had hurriedly ushered Ray from the house. Now inexplicably I was dreading it and I knew that this time there would be no postponement. Ray had risen to his feet and was standing across the table, waiting. He made no move towards me but to my helpless terror I found I was moving slowly and inexorably towards him. I had almost reached him by the time that I was able to force myself to stop, having to push back against an almost physical force which was propelling me forward. His eyes burned into mine and his face was glistening with sweat. He gave a breathless little laugh and reached for me avidly, his open mouth closing over mine. I stiffened, holding myself as far from him as I could, appalled that by walking round the table to meet him I had virtually invited the embrace.

After a moment I succeeded in wrenching my head away and his lips moved to my throat and the open neckline of my dress, hot and frighteningly insistent. In escalating panic I pushed against his chest with both hands and at last he raised his head and looked at me. He was breathing quickly and there was an ugly expression in his eyes.

'What's the matter? It's no use playing the ice maiden with me, my girl. You wanted that as much as I did.'

'No!' I shook my head desperately. 'No, Ray, please—'

'Then why did you come to me? You like to blow hot and cold, is that it? Egg someone on and then give him the deep freeze?'

'No,' I said again.

His mouth twisted. 'Don't fight me, Chloe. It won't do any good.'

The kitchen clock ticked unconcernedly into the suddenly threatening silence and I said on a high note of relief, 'Your free period's nearly over. You'd better go.'

He glanced impatiently at his watch. 'When can I see you, then? We'll keep Saturday for the sightseeing, but—'

I said quickly, 'Ray, I really think perhaps—'

'Hell, I'll have to go. We'll fix something at college tomorrow.'

'I shan't be there.'

'You will, my sweet, believe me.'

'But it's not one of Martha's days.'

He lifted a hand to caress my cheek, his smile fading as I ducked away. 'Goodbye, then, Chloe. For now.'

When he had gone I sank tremblingly on to the chair and put my hands to my face. On the table the untouched teapot still steamed. What in the name of heaven had happened to me? He was right, I had after all gone to him voluntarily—

No! I raised my head. Not voluntarily. Numbly I thought back to my first meeting with Ray and how, after initially ruling out any physical attraction towards him, I had almost been overwhelmed by it. Could the sensation have been deliberately imposed on me, overriding my own will? It was a terrifying thought but I of all people had reason not to underestimate the power of suggestion. This afternoon it had swamped me again, but if he

65

had relaxed his mental hold in the moment of physical contact, all my natural reserve would have come flooding back.

I drew a deep breath. If these hypotheses had any grain of truth in them, Hugo had been right to warn me about Ray, though he could have had no inkling how dangerous our liaison could be. 'Don't fight me,' Ray had said. 'It won't do any good.'

Hugo and Martha were full of praise for the chicken that evening, 'especially,' Hugo commented, 'since we were on starvation rations at lunch time. The girl who does the staff lunch has gone down with 'flu and so has her husband. Everything was chaotic—we had to make do with cheese and biscuits, if you please!'

'No wonder you're hungry,' I remarked, refilling the plate he held out. 'I didn't realize you have outside caterers.'

'Only for our lunch. The boys go back to their houses but for some reason lunches aren't provided in Staff House during the week. In any case the non-resident members don't want to trail home at midday, so I suppose it was considered easier to feed us all together.'

'Who has the contract?'

'The young married couple who run the restaurant down the road. It's only open in the evenings, so I imagine they're glad of the extra money providing our lunches five days a week.'

'It sounds just the kind of business I should be looking for!'

'I thought you didn't want to be burdened by overheads?'

I smiled. 'I was only trying not to run before I could walk. Anyway, I hope for your sakes order will be restored tomorrow.'

'I very much doubt it. Everyone was rushing round trying to persuade the cooks in the different houses to provide a bit extra for us but they all have different menus so it would be very complicated.'

I said on impulse, 'I could do the lunches till she's better, if it would help.'

Hugo looked up. 'Now that is a thought! Do you think you could cope?'

'I don't see why not. I'm used to cooking for fairly large numbers, and I've nothing else to do.'

'Bully for you! I'll ring through after dinner and pass on the suggestion.'

The college accepted my offer with gratitude as, when in turn I phoned her, did Annette St Cyr.

'This is the first time we've let St Olaf's down,' she told me, 'and I've been so worried it might lose us the contract. They must be able to depend on their caterers. That's the trouble with there being only two of us—when we're both ill we're completely stuck. We've had to cancel restaurant bookings till the end of the week, which is something we can't really afford.'

'Don't worry about the lunches, anyway. If you tell me what you were planning and where I can find it, I'll do the rest.'

'It should be Spaghetti Bolognese tomorrow, with ice-cream to follow. The sauce only needs thawing and reheating. The main problem is getting it to you.'

'I'll come and collect it, if there's somewhere you can leave it.'

'Would you mind? We could put the containers in the passage just inside the back door and leave it on the latch. We'll keep out of the way though—I don't want to pass this on to you! There's a large selection of pans at college, so don't worry about utensils. You know the kitchenette off the staff-room? It has a cooker, fridge, sink and so on. They use it to make tea and coffee during the day. The washing-up isn't your concern, of course. Two girls come in to serve the meal and clear and wash up afterwards. Once the dessert is portioned out you're free to go.'

I was quite pleased at the prospect of cooking again, having enjoyed the challenge of the *Poularde*, and it was only as I was dropping off to sleep that I realized I should in fact, as Ray had assured me, be at college the following day.

CHAPTER SIX

The Viking Restaurant was a converted coach-house on the Jurby road and Annette's clear directions led me to it without any trouble. The sign of a helmeted warrior with flowing hair dispelled any possible doubt that I had reached my destination. As arranged I walked round the building and pushed open the back door. The small passage inside obviously doubled as a wine cellar and racks of bottles lined the walls. There was a flight of stairs at the far end and on the left a door led presumably to the kitchen. I was tempted to take a quick peep inside but discretion overcame curiosity. I collected the containers left ready for me, snipped down the latch on the door and went on my way.

As I approached the corner where we'd seen the ram my hands tightened apprehensively on the driving-wheel, but today the fields and hillside falling away below me held no trace of strangeness. Perhaps the atmosphere was expunged of any lingering unease once the foreseen incident had taken place. I put it thankfully out of my mind and minutes later turned into the gateway of St Olaf's.

By the time the girls arrived to lay the long table everything was well in hand and for the next half-hour or so I worked harder than I had for some time, ladling steaming mounds of spaghetti and sauce on to a seemingly endless succession of plates.

'That's all for in there,' Kitty, the elder girl, said at last. 'These three plates are ours. We've just enough time to eat it before serving the sweet.'

We sat down at the small corner table and as we ate they regaled me with news of their boy-friends and their homes in the village. I gathered they spent the rest of the day helping with the housework at one of the college houses. Despite their chatter, however, they ate remarkably quickly and were pushing back their chairs before I had eaten half my own meal. I wasn't hungry anyway and abandoned it to embark on spooning out the ice-cream. Since I didn't want any myself I was then free to go. I said good-bye to the girls and, avoiding the still crowded staff-room, went out by the other door leading directly on to the corridor. I pulled it shut behind me and turned to find myself face to face with Ray. He took my arm.

'I've some sketches of the island to show you. They may give you an idea of where you'd like to go on Saturday.'

Before I could think of an excuse he led me firmly down the passage and into a small room with canvases stacked all round the walls. 'This is my private sanctum. I keep my equipment here, where it can be safely locked up. Some of it is quite valuable.'

Dubiously, with the idea of escape still at the forefront of my mind, I looked about me. On the easel at one end of the room was the half-completed portrait of an old woman and even I, with no knowledge of art, could see the expertise in the simple, telling strokes which had captured an impression of yearning loneliness. Interest overcame my hesitancy.

'That's wonderful, Ray! Who is she?'

'My grandmother. The family's pretty long-suffering about sitting for me. There are one or two sketches of them among the landscapes.'

He gestured towards the nearest pile of canvases and I started to flick through them: seascapes, an imposing mountain scene, the impudent face of a small boy, a man with penetrating eyes and a small goatee beard—

The canvases slithered to my feet in an untidy heap. Some corner of my mind noted Ray's stillness but my eyes were locked on the top canvas, a face I knew I should never be able to forget. 'Who—' My voice didn't sound the first time: patiently I tried again. 'Ray, who is that man?'

'Another relative.' His voice shook slightly. 'The black sheep of the family, in fact—my Uncle Tom.'

Black sheep—the ram darting into the road. I shook my head to clear it. 'Uncle Tom?' I repeated stupidly.

'That's right. Tom Kelly.'

My voice seemed no part of me. 'Is he—he's a hypnotist, isn't he?'

Ray let out his breath in a long sigh. 'He was once, yes.'

The walls of the little room tilted ominously. 'Could I sit down?'

'Of course.' He lifted an untidy pile of papers from the room's only chair and I lowered myself on to it, my hands tightening convulsively round the edge of the seat till the wood bit deeply into the palms. He stood watching me, the papers still in his arms. 'You're not going to pass out, are you?'

'I don't think so.'

'I had to do it, Chloe. I had to be sure.'

I dragged my eyes to his face. 'You mean you knew?'

'That you were the one he couldn't bring round? Yes.'

'How?' The word was only a whisper, as though I didn't really want an answer.

'We used to be pretty close, Uncle and I. I was over on the mainland when it happened and he phoned me in one hell of a flap asking what he should do. We'd had a game going between us for years—telepathy, hypnotism, all kinds of tests of will-power. He wanted me to join up with him as a double act but I was at art school by then and there seemed more security in carrying on with that.'

'You mean he wanted you to try to wake

72

me?'

'He didn't know what he wanted. He went to pieces completely. Nothing like that had ever happened before. By the time I got to Oxford he'd changed his mind and clammed up. Wouldn't tell me a thing about you, even your name. As you can imagine, having dropped everything to go to his assistance I was pretty rattled about it.' His eyes slid away from me. 'So I—muscled in on the act, as you might say.'

The silence between us was thick and suffocating. 'Go on,' I said.

'It was like bugging a phone, but as it turned out only partially successful. I think the old devil imposed a block somewhere along the line. I could get through to you all right, but nothing came back. It was maddening, knowing you were receiving but not your reactions. All that came over was a kind of quivering electrical response.'

He turned from me and lit a cigarette. 'We had one hell of a row about it. He knew I was tapping the current somewhere and he couldn't stop me. What really got him was that it was himself had taught me how.' He blew out a succession of smoke rings as I sat unmoving. 'I don't know why I went on with it; sheer bloody-mindedness, I suppose. At any rate every now and then, to prove to myself I could still call you up, I made contact, and gradually it got me hooked. I just had to find out who you were.' He paused again and again I remained silent.

'Uncle had gone to ground in some grotty little office in Chester. In spite of being cleared he wouldn't even contemplate hypnotism again and of course he wasn't trained for anything else. So I went to all the trouble of rooting him out but the stubborn old fool still wouldn't budge and of course your name had been kept out of the papers— protecting minors or something. So my only hope was to bring you to the island.'

It seemed imperative that I make some move to assert myself. My brain was reeling with implications too enormous to comprehend but I managed to say shakily, 'I came here to visit Hugo.'

He ignored the interruption. 'It's been a long wait. I was beginning to get desperate. Oh, there were a couple of false alarms— wishful thinking really—but when you did come I knew at once, even before I saw you.'

I closed my eyes, remembering the mental bombardment from the garden gate—and the little symbolic black cloud.

'Sometimes,' I said hastily, staring down again at my twisting fingers, 'I have very vivid dreams. I think they're set here and some of them seem to take place in the island's ancient past. Is that—do you—?'

He shook his head. 'Not guilty. You're probably receiving them direct from old Tom.

You're still linked to him, after all, and he's nuts about the place. When I was a kid we'd walk for hours out on the fells while he told me all the old legends about bugganes and phynnodderees and the rest. It was himself took me to see Granny Clegg. She's a weird old soul living down on the harbour at Peel, and what she doesn't know about the island isn't worth knowing at all.'

Granny Clegg. There would come a time when she might be able to help me—

I said sharply, 'It doesn't seem to occur to you that I might resent being taken over like this. Anyway, you've proved your point, or you seem to think you have, so will you please stop it now and let me go.'

'Let you go, is it?' There was a note in his voice which brought the gooseflesh to my skin. 'Now why should I do that? Haven't I only just succeeded in getting you here? No, I'll not let you go, Chloe, don't think it. You belong to me. Surely you can see that? I told you so yesterday.'

My heart lurched. The unexpected intrusion of Tom Kelly had momentarily blotted out the extent of my problem with Ray. Now I saw that this was deeper and more threatening than I could have imagined and to ward off the sudden personal element I said quickly, 'What did you mean about my still being linked to your uncle?'

'Well, it's obvious, isn't it? The connection

was never broken. O.K., you were brought round eventually, but by someone else. The particular line joining your mind and his was never cut and the dreams you mention seem to show something's still passing along it, like a telephone receiver that hasn't been replaced properly.'

Somewhere in another world a bell rang and the corridor outside echoed with hurrying feet. 'I must go,' I said mechanically.

There was a tap on the door and a boy put his head round. 'Excuse me, Mr Kittering, H.M.'s looking for you, sir.'

'Right, thanks.' He glanced at me as I rose unsteadily to my feet. 'I'm afraid I'll have to leave you, and we still haven't fixed anything for Saturday.'

'I really think I'd rather—' But he had already taken my arm and opened the door and we emerged to see Neil coming down the corridor towards us. I stopped abruptly, pulling Ray to a halt.

'So there you are.' Neil spoke directly to me. 'Hugo said you were here somewhere.' He frowned slightly, searching my face. 'Are you all right, Chloe? You're very pale.'

'I'll have to go,' Ray interrupted. 'I'll phone you this evening.'

He walked quickly away down the corridor and Neil said gently, 'You don't look overjoyed at the prospect.'

I moistened my lips. 'I think I've had

76

enough of him for one day.'

'Then come out somewhere with me instead.'

I stared at him uncomprehendingly, still trying to shake myself free of the clinging strands of fear, and he smiled, his mouth going up in the way that somewhere deep inside myself I remembered so well. 'That doesn't seem to strike you as a much better alternative!'

'I'm sorry,' I said with an effort. 'I'd like to, thank you.'

'Fine. Do you play squash?'

It was difficult for me to adjust to what he was saying. 'I haven't for a while, but I used to.'

'Would you like a game, then? We've some quite good courts here. If Martha could kit you up I can provide a racket.' His eyes moved assessingly over my face. 'You're sure you're all right?'

'Yes, really.'

'I'll have to go; I'm due to invigilate but I'll put my name down for a court on the way and pick you up about eight.'

The air outside was sweet and clear and cold after the stuffy central heating in college. I stood drawing in lungsful of it before I climbed into Martha's little Ford and set off for home.

Tom Kelly. I'd forgotten he was a Manxman, but now I remembered the jingle

77

that had been his signature tune—'Kelly from the Isle of Man'. And there was another tune—but it was dangerous to think of that.

He loved this island, Ray had said, was sure to know the legend of Sigurd and Fafni, about the strange gatherings on the mound and the dance on the seashore.

Somehow I had reached the cottage. Martha came out to meet me as I climbed unsteadily out of the car. 'How did it go?'

I looked at her blankly.

'The lunch, girl! Did you manage all right?'

'Oh—yes, I think so, thanks.' I felt a deep need to confide in her, to share the mounting fears of my unwilling involvement with Ray, but she and Hugo would simply prevent my seeing him and I knew that wasn't the answer. Running away from his phone call this evening was a temporary respite, no more. I now knew that the unaccountable phenomena that had been assailing me ever since I came to the island had their roots five years in the past, and I suspected that I shouldn't be free of them until they had played themselves out to the end.

Martha, delighted to learn of my date with Neil, willingly lent me her plimsolls and tennis whites and as he'd promised Neil brought one or two rackets for me to choose from. Fortunately I managed to give him quite a good game. There was relief in physical exercise, in slamming the ball and

78

concentrating on it to the exclusion of all else. When our time was up Neil slipped a casual arm round my shoulders as we walked from the court.

'Well done! I enjoyed that—we must do it again.'

It was only then that some movement on the shadowed balcony overlooking the court made me glance up with an instinctive fear of finding Ray looking down on me. But it was Pam Beecham who dodged back out of sight and I released my indrawn breath. I don't think Neil saw her; in any event he made no comment and nor did I.

'I could of course offer you an exotic cup of cocoa at Staff House,' he said as I joined him again outside the changing-rooms, 'but personally I feel a glass of something at the King Orry might be more acceptable.'

I hesitated. 'Does Ray ever go there?'

'Not as far as I know. I've never seen him. Has he been bothering you in some way, because I can soon—'

'No,' I said hastily, 'it's nothing like that.'

'I gather Hugo's not too happy about your seeing him,' he remarked as he opened the car door.

'Why, what did he say?'

'Oh, nothing specific, it was just an impression I had. I can't say I blame him though. You looked really shaken at lunch time. What is it between you two?'

79

'I can't explain,' I said helplessly, 'at least, not at the moment. If I tried to you wouldn't believe me.'

'Apparently I'm not to be given the chance. Still, if you prefer not to talk about it, fair enough. I just thought it might help.'

The King Orry was quieter than it had been on Sunday and we found a corner settle near the huge old fireplace. Several times I caught Neil's eyes consideringly on my face, but he didn't question me any further and our conversation was light and general. I was tired after the physical exertion and the mental traumas of the day and soon after ten he said, 'I think I'd better take you home, young lady, before you fall asleep in your chair.'

We didn't speak much on the way back and at the cottage he got out and opened the gate for me. 'Thanks for the game and the drink,' I said dutifully.

'My pleasure. And Chloe—'

'Yes?'

'Take care.' For a moment his eyes held mine. Then I nodded, attempted a not very successful smile, and turned to walk up the path to the house.

CHAPTER SEVEN

It was bitterly cold. A thin icy wind was blowing straight in from the sea, lancing through my threadbare skirt and the shawl I wrapped tightly about my shoulders. Around me, people stamped their feet and rubbed their raw red hands together for warmth, but the despair in their eyes was not for their own discomfort.

'The King'll not let it happen,' the woman beside me said suddenly. ' 'Tis old history now and Her Ladyship came to no harm. Wasn't it the Island he was thinking of, and no wrong in that?'

'Master George'll explain,' a man answered reassuringly. 'There may still be time.'

But even as he spoke a shudder ran through the crowd, and straining over the heads in front of me I could make out a figure escorted by guards being helped up on to the little mound. The woman beside me fell to her knees keening in a high-pitched whine which, together with the strong wind, made it exceedingly difficult to hear the prisoner's final speech. But he was standing straight and true and through my streaming tears I saw that white blankets covered the hillock so that not a drop of his blood should soak away into the ground.

As the shots rang out the scene wavered and starred like a shattered mirror, but down the long years its lament still reached me: 'Dty vaaish, Illiam Dhone, te brishney nyn gree— Thy death, Illiam Dhone, is breaking our heart.'

* * *

With a sigh, I spooned out the last helpings of blackcurrant sponge and loaded them on to the tray Kitty held ready. The unexplained phenomenon I'd experienced in the early hours of the morning had left me decidedly on edge—my second excursion into the past in the space of a couple of days. I was unable to dismiss it simply as a dream, however special, even though I had not, as on the last occasion, been wide awake immediately beforehand. In fact I had been lying drowsily in the limbo between sleep and waking remembering the evening spent with Neil. Then, suddenly, the anxious crowds and the cold wind blowing.

'Where the hell were you last night?'

I jumped and turned to meet Ray's belligerent gaze. The word 'Ronaldsway' came instinctively to my mind but I blocked it off and answered as levelly as I could, 'Playing squash.'

'You knew I was going to phone.'

'But you didn't say what time. Did you expect me to wait in all evening?'

'I certainly didn't realize I had to queue for your favours!' His eyes held mine, furious but with an underlying bewilderment which, to my consternation, I found rather touching. He had obviously expected my instant capitulation to whatever plans he had for me, and the first hint of defiance left him floundering.

'Anyway,' I added more calmly, 'it was only to make arrangements for Saturday, wasn't it?' And I realized as I spoke that my brief moment of sympathy had irrevocably committed me to a full day in his company.

He stared at me a moment longer, his mouth still sulky, then he relaxed. 'O.K. Ten o'clock suit you?'

'I'll be ready.'

Neil didn't come to the kitchen to see me. There was, of course, no reason why he should. Once as the door swung to behind one of the hurrying girls I caught a quick, unwelcome picture of him sitting beside Pam, their heads together laughing at something. Either she had forgiven him for the previous evening's defection or she was taking extra care that it shouldn't happen again.

I tugged off my apron and hung it on its hook. The tight band round my head was threatening to turn into a full-scale migraine and the lingering smell of food in the small room added to my malaise.

With a sense of relief I pulled the door to the quadrangle shut behind me, welcoming the cool breeze on my face. Directly opposite a stone archway led through the science wing to the college gardens and, unwilling to face the immediate prospect of the car journey home, I made my way towards it, emerging from the shadowed archway into brilliant sunshine. The playing-fields stretched away to my left behind the assembly hall and I could see a few boys in the distance kicking a ball about before the game began. Ahead of me, beyond the stretch of neat lawns and flowerbeds, the five boarding-houses stood in a row like ancient guardians. I stood for a moment looking across at them, but the sunlight was too strong for my aching eyes and flowers, grass and glinting grey stone merged into a blinding kaleidoscope.

I was just deciding to return to the car after all when the sound of footsteps made me turn in the sudden hope that Neil might be hurrying after me. But it was John Stevens who joined me with a smile.

'I believe we have you to thank for saving us from the rigours of starvation? On behalf of us all, much thanks!'

Automatically I fell into step beside him. 'It's a pleasure. I'm quite enjoying it.'

'Confidentially, there's been a distinct improvement in cuisine the last couple of days! Annette St Cyr's a nice little thing but it's her husband who's the real chef and he keeps well away!'

The path we were walking along had been winding its way between the sweeping lawns but now it divided, one fork leading to the houses and the other back in the direction of the main gates. John hesitated.

'Are you making for anywhere in particular?'

'No, just trying to shake off a headache.'

'Oh, bad luck. I'd better leave you then. I have to collect a couple of books from Staff House and class begins in five minutes.'

He set off down the path and I had started along the other one when suddenly, with an incredulous shaft of fear, I seemed to see him lying on the ground covered in blood.

I spun round, wide-eyed. He was still in sight walking quickly away from me. I tried to call out but no sound came. He had almost reached the house and a clock in my head started on an ominous count-down to disaster.

Frantically I hurled myself forward over the grass, my feet seeming hardly to move as I fought my way through the sudden density of the atmosphere. Stop! I shrieked silently. Don't go any further! Wait! But he didn't stop, or even look round until, just short of the shallow step leading to the porch, he became aware of my pursuit and turned in surprise. By then it was already too late. With a last superhuman burst of speed I flung myself against him and we fell together against the heavy wood of the front door. In the same

85

instant a deafening crash exploded immediately behind us and as the clouds of dust rose we could make out the shattered remains of a huge chimney lying on the path. John's hands were gripping my shoulders, his face above mine suddenly ashen.

'My God, that was a close thing! If you hadn't—'

Beside us the front door burst open and people came hurrying out to see what had happened, gasping and exclaiming at our escape.

'It was Chloe!' John said jerkily. 'She saved my life. If she hadn't pushed me clear—'

Everyone clustered round, congratulating me on noticing the sudden danger, and I had almost convinced myself that no-one would suspect the truth when a couple of workmen, white-faced, pushed their way through the small throng.

'Anybody hurt? Thank God for that! There was nothing we could do—it just suddenly toppled and fell.'

Someone said importantly, 'Fortunately this young lady saw it in time,' and I held my breath.

The workman turned to me. 'You saw it, Miss? But how could you? It wouldn't have been in sight until it was actually on its way down!'

'And I left you at the fork in the path,' John put in excitedly. 'To have reached me in time, you must have started running well before the chimney began to fall!'

There was a sudden startled silence and a dozen pairs of eyes fastened on me almost fearfully. I said limply, 'I just—thought something might happen.'

'It was the hand of fate!' asserted the second workman, crossing himself. 'Your time had not yet come.'

John took my hand. 'Chloe, how did you know? Can you explain it?'

'Not really. I had a sudden—impression of you lying hurt, that's all.'

A woman in a white overall pushed her way forward. 'I'm Matron, my dear. I think perhaps it would be advisable if you came and lay down for a while.'

I shook my head. 'No, really, thank you. I'm all right and my sister-in-law will be expecting me.'

John said awkwardly, 'It seems so inadequate to say thank you.'

'There's no need, anyway. In the circumstances, what else could I have done?'

How far back, I wondered, did the chain of coincidence stretch? I'd decided on a walk only because of the headache, which in turn had been caused by my experiences during the night. Had it all been elaborately designed in order to save John Stevens's life?

'You're late,' Martha remarked when I eventually arrived back at the cottage.

'Just another touch of E.S.P.,' I said wearily, and told her what had happened.

'The ram the other day and now this. It seems to be stepping up, doesn't it? It'll certainly give them something to talk about in the staff-room!'

Dully I wondered what Neil would make of it. And Ray—

Hugo was full of questions when he arrived home. 'What's all this about your life-saving act? It's got St Olaf's by the ears, principally because there seems to have been no logical way you could have known of the danger.'

He listened carefully as I gave him the brief facts. 'And that's all? You've no idea what alerted you to it?'

'Pure instinct, I suppose.'

'Precognition, more like.' He looked at me closely. 'It's not the first time, is it? Is this another legacy from your hypnotist friend?'

'Possibly,' I replied steadily, 'but it wasn't really precognition this time. I "saw" John lying on the ground covered in blood, and that didn't happen.'

'It probably would have done if you hadn't intervened. So much for predestination.'

'Perhaps it was clairvoyance, then?' Martha suggested. 'After all, the fault in the chimney was presumably already there. Chloe sensed it and subconsciously deduced what was likely to happen.'

Hugo sighed and stood up. 'Well, don't

88

make a habit of this kind of thing or we'll have to hire a booth and set you up in business on Douglas Pier!'

I tried to smile but his obvious disquiet had only strengthened my resolve not to confide in him more fully. As I'd suspected, the more extravagant of my mental wanderings would have to be kept to myself for the time being.

CHAPTER EIGHT

My see-sawing emotions were no steadier when Ray called for me as arranged the next morning, and perhaps gauging my turbulent mood he made no mention of the incident which must have been uppermost in his mind.

'I thought we'd go down through Kirk Michael and Glen Helen to St John's,' he said as we turned in the direction of Ballaugh. 'We can have a look at Tynwald Hill and then take the mountain road down to the south-west tip.' He slowed to negotiate a flock of sheep which, with an alert dog at their heels, were moving down the road ahead of us.

'I'd like to show you Cregneish. The Folk Museum will be closed now the season's over but you can still see the typical Manx cottages, all thatched and whitewashed, and there's a grand view from there over the Calf. There's a bit of Norse for you, by the way: islets alongside a larger island are known in Scandinavian as calves.'

'Is there much Scandinavian influence left on the island?' Unwillingly I was remembering my dream of the tall fair men thronging the hillside. It hadn't escaped me that they very closely resembled the sign outside the Viking Restaurant.

'A fair bit, especially in the north, though the culture is basically Celtic. Half the surnames on the island are Norse, my own included. Most of them begin with Q, K or a hard C. Incidentally, one of the most common is Christian. Fletcher Christian of the *Bounty* mutiny was a Manxman.' *And Illiam Dhone—*

'This is Bishopscourt, on the right here. You can't see much of it from the road. Part of it was built in the twelve hundreds and it's been the official residence of the Bishop of Sodor and Man for centuries, though the present bishop lives elsewhere, which seems a shame.'

Kirk Michael awaited us, with its palm trees lining the road, its deep blue water and pretty houses. 'There's the Irish coastline across the water,' Ray pointed out. 'You'll be seeing England and Scotland too, if the weather stays clear. We're right in the centre of the British Isles. They say from the top of Snaefell you can see six kingdoms: England, Ireland, Scotland, Wales, Man, and the Kingdom of Heaven!'

The road was lined with hedges of prickly

gorse and hips and haws glowed redly like a scattering of rubies. Above us fluffy white clouds raced across the blue sky. Ray's naturalness was having its effect; for the first time I was actually enjoying his company and as I relaxed I felt the stirring of a long-dormant love for this sturdily independent little island.

The road started to climb and on either side the fields fell away criss-crossed by gorse hedges, with cattle and sheep grazing peacefully and plumes of smoke rising from the farmhouses, and as we drove, Ray recounted odd snatches of history and folklore as they came into his head, about Mannanan the Magician who had lived on South Barrule and used to throw a cloak of mist round the island whenever strangers approached.

'He couldn't hide it from St Patrick, though, and when the people began to pay tribute to him and his monks instead of to Mannanan, the magician turned himself into three legs joined together and rolled like a wheel down the hill. We still talk of Mannanan drawing his cloak when the mist comes down.'

The road was now hemmed in by thickly wooded hillsides and a river cascaded on our left. In the autumn sunlight the trees were a riot of rich colour—spruce and fir, oak, sycamore and beech. 'Glen Helen,' Ray told me as I exclaimed in delight. A few minutes later we had left the glen behind us and were approaching St John's. 'You know about Tynwald, of course?'

'Only that it's a parliament independent of Westminster.'

'And the oldest continuous government in the world,' Ray said with quiet pride. 'It's been in existence over a thousand years.' We came up the road past the cattle market into St John's and his voice blurred in my ears as I found myself gazing with a kind of numb resignation at the oddly shaped hillock of my dream. So today was not to be an escape after all.

'It was a site of Celtic sun-worship even before the Vikings,' Ray was explaining. 'The four tiers of the hill are made up of soil from the seventeen parishes of Man, symbolizing the entire island. On Old Midsummer Day every year the laws are read out here in English and Manx Gaelic.' Was it Manx, then, the language in my dream that I had not been able to identify?

The echoes of that dream were all about me, the heat that suffused me no part of this cool October day but burning down from a sun which had set a thousand years ago. The murmur of voices and the clank of swords formed a continuous undercurrent to Ray's voice as he parked the car and led me up the stone steps to the topmost tier.

'The sun-worship bit is still there if you look for it. The ceremony takes place at noon with the sun directly overhead and the dignitaries face to the east. It's hard to know where one culture ends and another begins.' He went on talking about Keys and Deemsters and I wondered dizzily how many of the vibrations which were bombarding me came directly from the folk memory of Tom Kelly the hypnotist and how many were channelled through his nephew at my side. And as Ray's actual presence came to the forefront of my mind, I became aware that he was standing watching me with a look of expectant excitement.

'You're getting something, aren't you?'

His face came back into focus and the past, throbbing with heat and pageantry, receded into its own wraiths.

'I knew Uncle's influence was bound to come out here!' There was an exultant note in his voice and immediately all my fears came rushing back. His easy charm that morning had deceived me into relaxing my guard so that he could prove to his satisfaction the bonds that still held me. Martha had warned me not to trust Ray.

I pulled away and ran ahead of him down the steps but he caught up with me before I reached the foot of the hill. 'Surely you can see what a breakthrough this is! Five years, for Pete's sake, and from the way you were acting up there, you're as much under his spell now as you were on that stage!'

I shuddered. 'That's not true! I shouldn't

93

think he knows anything about it.'

'For sure he doesn't. He's not done any mind-reading since and like any gift it fades if you don't use it. But that's the wonder of it, don't you see, that just the residual influence is enough to produce the dreams and the premonition you had yesterday. God, the possibilities it opens up!'

I started to shiver violently as though I had in truth emerged from the heat of summer into this cool autumn morning. He caught hold of my arm, spinning me round to face him. 'What was it that you saw up there? What era— Vikings, or the Horsemen of the Parishes riding in procession?' His eyes were burning into mine as though he could read my mind at will. 'Chloe, for God's sake! I've got to know!'

I pulled myself free and started back towards the car and, swearing under his breath, he came after me. 'It's stepping up,' Martha had said, and Hugo: 'Another legacy from the hypnotist?' Now Ray assumed without question that the dreams, the premonition about John and the ghosts of Tynwald came to me directly from the mind of Tom Kelly. If they were all right and my mind was really so firmly welded to his, were any of its thoughts my own?

I knew, as he slammed the car door, that Ray was annoyed with me for remaining silent but I felt unable to justify myself to him. These last few minutes had been a new experience, a strange half and half world of the past impinging on the present without a total time slip. I went over them again and again, probing and analysing, and it was some minutes before I began to distinguish a new uneasiness, a deepening sense of despair which weighed increasingly down on me until it was almost unbearable.

Apprehensively I looked out of the window to find some reason for it, but we were driving along a pretty road halfway up a hill and the glorious foliage was with us still, lit to rust, bronze and gold in the thick sunshine. But whether there was any reason or none for my misery I found I couldn't stand it. I put my hands suddenly over my ears. 'I don't like this place! Let's go back!'

Ray didn't answer and when I glanced at him I saw the gleam of satisfaction in his eyes.

'Please, Ray! I'm frightened!' If he wanted me to beg I was prepared to do so, anything to get away from the appalling sense of doom which was now overpowering me. He smiled slightly and I realized with a shock that my distress was being inflicted deliberately, as a punishment for resisting him.

If he refused to help me I must somehow escape by myself. With a sob of terror I wrenched open the car door but he leaned across me and slammed it shut again. 'All right, all right, I'll take you down.'

'What's that noise?' I demanded as he

turned the car on the narrow road. 'That distant rumbling? It sounds like thunder.'

He was still smiling and for the first time I saw cruelty openly on his face. Charming and attractive he could be, as long as he was getting his way, but below the surface lay a more unpleasant side of his nature—the one, no doubt, which Martha had admitted frightened her.

'I can't hear anything,' he said.

So the noise too was for me alone, together with the terror and pain which were darkening my mind. I gripped the sides of the seat and shut my eyes tightly, willing myself to keep calm, and as we moved away down the hill the suffocating horror gradually ebbed until I was able to breathe more easily. Back on the main road Ray stopped the car and lit a cigarette.

'What was that place?' I asked in a whisper.

'Slieu Whallian, the witches' hill.' For all his apparent detachment his voice shook slightly. 'Women suspected of witchcraft were put in spiked barrels and rolled down it. If they were dead when they reached the bottom it was considered to be divine judgement, if they were alive, proof of their powers and they were burned at the stake. At least, that's how the story goes. A medieval case of "Heads I win, tails you lose".'

After a long moment I said, 'If I'd been living in those days I'd probably have suffered the same fate.'

'Are you going to tell me this time what you felt?'

'Sheer terror,' I said flatly, 'and difficulty in breathing.'

'The rumble you mentioned would have been the barrels rolling.'

I looked at his pitiless face with a kind of sick horror and the expression in his eyes changed as he reached for me. 'I warned you not to fight me, my darling. I can punish you if I have to, but it shouldn't be necessary.'

His mouth blocked off my protest and since he was stronger than I, I lay rigidly in his arms, emotionally uninvolved in his kisses. Only when I felt his hand fumbling at my breast did I put up my own to intercept it and turn my face away.

'Now what's the matter?' he demanded unevenly.

'That's enough, and it's no use threatening me again.' I sat up and pushed back my hair. 'Don't make the mistake of thinking I'll submit to anything for fear of being "punished" as you call it. What's the penalty for refusing to kiss you, anyway? A visit to Cronk-ny-arrey-lhaa?' I broke off, seeing his eyes widen. 'There— isn't such a place, is there?' The name had come into my mind without thought.

'Indeed there is, a Viking burial mound. What's more, you pronounced it perfectly. Perhaps I need a yellow flower in my buttonhole after all.'

Protection against witchcraft—'It's your own fault,' I said shakily, 'you deliberately triggered it off.'

'But you brought it on yourself, didn't you now? You were being rather stubborn, my love, and I felt it was time for a demonstration of how the land lay. I think you'll agree it was effective.'

'So far,' I said slowly, 'you've always had the advantage of surprise. Now that I know what you're trying to do you'll find it isn't so easy.'

He gave a short laugh. 'A challenge, is it? Right, my lovely, we'll see who's the stronger. Now, do we call a truce and go on with the tour?'

'Only if you promise to abide by it and not attempt any more take-overs.'

'Take-overs,' he repeated slowly. 'A good description, that, though I'd prefer to think of it as a merger; a complete merger, body, mind and soul. How does that strike you, Chloe Winter?'

I shook my head. 'Out of the question.'

'We'll see, we'll see. Now, after all this mind-bending I'm sure you're in need of a bite of lunch. Don't look so wary, my love! I won't play any more games with you today.'

So we stopped for lunch at an isolated little inn and then drove on along Foxdale and down the Sloc road through bleak mountain stretches with Soph Barrule towering over us and thickly wooded plantations on every side.

And Ray, his good humour restored, started again on snippets of folklore—about the Rider of Sloc, the Benvarreys or mermaids round the coast, the fearful Tarroo-ushtay that lived up in the Curraghs and the Nightman who blew on his bugle before a storm.

But though I listened to his stories and made comments where expected, I couldn't forget that a challenge had been offered and accepted, and while Ray regarded it simply as an exciting contest, for myself it was a question of survival.

On the hillside below Cregneish we stood looking across the sound at the low-lying Calf and the half-submerged rocks known as Kitterland and Ray told me the story of the drowned Norwegian baron they commemorated. 'And we have our own Atlantis lying out there somewhere,' he added. 'Fishermen say it rises up sometimes in the morning mist. It was once an island as big as Man, inhabited by a three-legged race who came across here on raids. Do you know the motto of the three legs, by the way? "Whichever way you throw me, I stand". Very appropriate, wouldn't you say, since the island's been tossed about between the Scots, the Vikings and the English and still retains its independence.'

We turned back to the car and I knew there was a question I had to ask in spite of myself. 'Isn't there a legend about Lugh the Harpist?'

He glanced at me sharply. 'Back to Uncle Tom?'

'When he put us into the trance he played something he called Lugh's Sleeping Tune.'

'That's right. Lugh of the Long Arm was the son of Kian, who ruled Erin, and was sent over here to be educated with Mannanan's sons. He became a great harpist and played three wonderful tunes, the Laughing Tune, the Sleeping Tune and the Weeping Tune. I'd have to check the details with Granny Clegg, but I think his country was invaded and he went back to defend it, armed with Mannanan's sword The Answerer.'

'It's a pity he didn't have a Waking Tune,' I said ruefully.

We were silent as we drove back past Port St Mary clustering round its little bay and on to the ancient capital of Castletown. Something about the brooding castle and dark, narrow streets depressed me and suddenly I was longing for the warmth of Hugo's fire and curtains drawn against the approach of darkness.

'Hadn't we better be making our way back?' I asked tentatively. 'It'll be getting dark soon and we shan't be able to see much anyway.'

'I'd thought we could have dinner somewhere.'

'Martha's expecting me for a meal and I am rather tired.'

'Just as you like. By the way, I meant what I

said about painting you. Out on the hills somewhere. I have a place in mind, not far from Ballacarrick.'

'How long would it take?'

'Two or three sittings, perhaps, a couple of hours at a time. I've a feeling it could be the best thing I've done.'

'But I'll only be here for another week.' As I spoke my mind went unbidden to Neil.

'Do you never listen to what I tell you? Didn't I say the day we met you'd be here a long time? Don't be thinking you'll escape me that easily!'

An apprehensive shiver ran down my spine. 'You can say what you like,' I declared roundly, 'but one more week is my limit. After that I must go back and decide how I'm going to set about earning my living.'

'I'll not argue with you. I've a free day every second Tuesday and it falls next week. Shall we make a start then, weather permitting?'

I hesitated. The thought of being alone with Ray on a deserted hilltop was not enticing but a numb kind of acceptance was closing over my mind and somehow I felt that this had to be and it was useless to try to avoid it.

'All right,' I said, 'provided Annette St Cyr is well enough to do the lunch by then.'

We drove up the mountain road, dropped down into Ramsey and so through Sulby to Ballacarrick. The shadow of the hills crept closer as evening approached. Winter was coming too, I thought with a touch of sadness. There were drifts of leaves lying in the gutters like spendthrift gold and by the corner of the old school house two small boys were trundling a grotesque-looking guy in a wheelbarrow. Tonight the clocks would go back an hour. The long-drawn-out concession to summer was coming to an end.

'When will I see you?' Ray asked as we drew up outside the cottage.

'Tuesday will be quite soon enough.' I reached for the door handle but he gripped my arm.

'Come on, now. You'll not be going without a goodnight kiss.'

I bent forward swiftly and kissed him on the mouth. 'Good-night, Ray. Thanks for showing me round.' And before he could stop me, I slid quickly out of the car.

He leaned across the passenger seat and looked up at me. 'The truce is over Chloe. From now on it's each of us for himself. O.K.?'

'O.K.'

He started the car and I stood looking after him until the red tail-light turned the corner and disappeared from sight.

CHAPTER NINE

We went to the college chapel the next morning as Martha had promised, and sitting with the staff in the gallery were able to look down on the serried rows of unusually tidy boys in their Sunday uniform. The building was Gothic in style and the stained glass window above the altar reminded me of Holman Hunt's famous picture *The Light of the World*.

But despite the deep peacefulness of the atmosphere and the sweetness of the boys' voices, I found it impossible to anchor my thoughts. There was too much in my mind of pre-Christian folklore on this sunny morning for the comfortable words of the Prayer Book to reach me, and though I joined in the familiar hymns my thoughts continued to circle round Celtic burial grounds, sun-worship and the lovely hillside above St John's, where the atmosphere was still charged with terror after three hundred long years.

I was also aware that several of those near us had been giving me curious looks, and I wasn't anxious to linger after the service but a group had gathered at the door and as we passed Simon Fenton called, 'Shall we be seeing you all at the King Orry this evening?'

Hugo paused. 'Possibly. We haven't really

thought about it yet.'

'Well, the gang will be there, if you can make it. You coming, Pam?'

Pam Beecham flung me a spiteful glance. 'Yes, Neil and I'll probably go along as usual.'

And it happened again. I heard myself say urgently, 'Don't go out this evening, Pam, please!'

Everyone turned to me in surprise and Pam regarded me open-mouthed.

'Well, I must say—!'

'I mean it. Whatever happens, please stay in. It's desperately important.'

'I've heard some things in my time, but really!'

'Listen, there'll be a phone call—a vital one. You'll never forgive yourself if you're not there.'

She continued to stare at me and I saw the uncertainty in her eyes. After a moment she said jerkily, 'You're turning into a regular little sybil, aren't you? And what *is* this phone call, may I ask? Tell me now and I needn't bother staying in!'

The urgency drained out of me as suddenly as it had arisen. 'I don't know,' I said dully. 'I just know it's terribly important.'

'Better listen to her, Pam!' Carol said with an uneasy laugh. 'She was right about John.'

'Nonsense, it was just a fluke. I don't believe a word of it.'

I shrugged and turned away, anxious now to

escape from the curiosity on their faces. Pam came after me and said in a low voice, 'I suppose you think if I cry off this evening Neil'll ask you instead? Sorry, my dear, you'll have to be a bit less obvious than that!'

I said wearily, 'You're wrong, Pam, but it's up to you. I've tried to warn you, that's all. If you won't listen there's nothing more I can do.'

Martha came up and took my arm. 'Come on, love, we left a joint in the oven, don't forget!' And she guided me swiftly back to the car.

'You really meant that, didn't you?' Hugo said as we drove out of the gates.

'It just suddenly came into my head.'

'And you don't know what this phone call would be about?'

'No.'

'Well, you're certainly livening things up around here, I must say!' But his eyes in the driving mirror were troubled and I regretted the compulsion which had once again forced me to make an exhibition of myself.

'Martha, who was Illiam Dhone?' I asked suddenly during lunch.

'William Christian—Brown-haired William. Did Ray mention him? He's by way of being the Manx national hero.'

'What—happened to him?'

'He was shot for treason on Hango Hill, though it seems he was innocent. The Earl of

Derby trumped up charges against him.'

'*A prompted and threatened jury*'—the few words I had caught.

'When was that?'

'His alleged offences were during the Civil War but he wasn't shot till 1663. The King's pardon arrived just too late to save him.'

1663. Had I slipped so completely into that year that the national grief had become mine, his death, as the ballad had it, broken my own heart? And was this just one more legacy from Tom Kelly?

'I think I'll go for a walk this afternoon,' I said abruptly.

'By yourself?' queried my shrewd brother.

'If you wouldn't mind. There are a few things I need to make my mind up about.'

I felt their exchanged glances, but all Martha said was, 'Try Tholt-y-Will, then, in Sulby Glen. The scenery's superb. It's quite a way from here but we can run you to the top and leave one of the cars lower down for you to make your way back to.'

Later that afternoon I was glad I had accepted her suggestion. Sulby Glen was spectacular indeed. The road wound through a narrow tunnel of trees which gradually opened out until we were running along one side of a widening valley. On our right the hill rose steeply from the road, thickly covered with gorse and bracken above which the closely packed trunks of majestic pines and firs towered overhead blotting out the sweep of mountainside. On the left the ground fell steeply away to the floor of the valley, where the torrents of centuries cascading down the face of the mountain had eaten into the rock causing an enormous fissure. On one side of this a waterfall still fell, swelling the quickly flowing river at its foot and creaming round the pile of jagged rocks and slate which formed a natural dam. Above this dramatic foreground whitewashed cottages perched precariously amid the folds of the hillside and low walls of Manx stone ran over the greenness which was liberally dotted with the snowflakes of grazing sheep.

At the inn halfway up we waited while Martha, who'd been following behind in her car, parked it in the forecourt and came to join us. 'Here are the keys. I think you'll have had enough by the time you get back here.'

'I'm sure you're right!' I commented, peering up the steepening road ahead of us. A few minutes later we came out at the top of the glen. To the left a grey stone wall curved away screening the view down the valley and ahead of us the ground levelled off into patches of scrubby gorse and bracken. Hugo stopped the car and pointed out a gate in the wall.

'That's the way you go. It's fairly steep on the way down, so be careful.'

'I will. Thanks for the lift.' The wind

whipped my hair stingingly across my face as I got out of the car. With a wave Hugo turned back down the glen and I manoeuvred my way through the gate. A breathtaking panorama met my eyes, fold after fold of rounded hills blazing with different coloured trees and sweeping stretches of rust bracken. The air was full of the noise of rushing water.

'Hello,' said Neil Sheppard.

I spun from my contemplation of the view and saw a wooden bench set back against the wall, from which he had risen. 'All by yourself?'

'Yes.'

He came over and stood beside me, staring out to where the sea lay between the farthest hills. 'It's magnificent, isn't it? I often come up here on a Sunday afternoon. A little solitude is very salutary now and again; there's not much opportunity for it at college.'

'I'm sorry if I'm encroaching.'

'Not at all, I'm delighted to share it with you. Were Hugo and Martha too lazy to come?'

'I'm afraid I rather discouraged them. I felt in need of some solitude myself.'

'Then you won't want me butting in. I'll walk back down the road.'

'No, please. I didn't mean that. It's just that I've been putting off making a few decisions and it seemed time I tackled them.'

'About Ray?' His eyes were still on the distance.

108

'Some of them.'

'He was holding forth at the inn before lunch on the joys of your day out together.'

My heart blundered into my ribs. 'What did he say?'

'Oh, that you were kindred spirits, perfectly in tune with one another and so on. It was very touching.'

'But hardly true,' I said in a low voice.

'Oh?'

'Would you say,' I began after a moment, 'that it's possible for a person to be completely subjugated to the will of someone else?' I felt him turn to stare at me but I kept my eyes on the distant hills.

'That's a loaded question for a Sunday afternoon! Hypnotism, you mean?'

'Its after-effects, really. Do you know anything about it?'

'Very little, I'm afraid.' He paused. 'Are we still talking about Ray?'

'Partly. It's a long story.'

'Then let's sit down and hear it in comfort.'

The bench was warm in the sunshine, sheltered from the stiff breeze on the other side of the wall. I said apologetically, 'This isn't what you came up here for. You've still time to escape, you know, before I "hold you with my glittering eye".'

He smiled. 'I've no wish to. It sounds most intriguing. You say hypnotism comes into it. Hugo mentioned that you had rather an

109

alarming experience a few years ago.'

'When did he tell you that?'

'On Friday, when we heard about you and John. He seemed to think there was some connection, that perhaps the long spell of unconsciousness had paved the way for a tendency to—E.S.P., don't they call it?'

'What Hugo doesn't know,' I said slowly, 'is that the hypnotist is Ray's uncle.'

'Ray Kittering's? Good Lord, what a coincidence!'

'No, that's the whole point—it isn't. Ray used to practise hypnotism and telepathy with his uncle and he claims that he—cut in somewhere along the line. He says that since his uncle didn't bring me round himself, the connection between us has never been broken.'

'Are you trying to tell me that Ray has some kind of mental hold over you?'

I didn't answer directly. 'He considers he's responsible for bringing me to the island.'

Neil stared at me. 'Responsible in what way?'

'Telepathically.'

'My God!'

'How far are you prepared to suspend your disbelief?'

'Try me.'

'Well, since I came here things have escalated fantastically. Over the last few years I've been having a series of vivid dreams which seemed to be set here, though I'd never been before. I recognized Tynwald Hill, for example. No, it's no use saying I'd seen photographs and forgotten them—and anyway, it's much more than that now. I—I actually seem to slip into the past.'

I turned to him with a half smile. 'I'm sorry, Neil, I know this is a lot more than you bargained for. The point is I've got to the stage when I have to tell someone and Hugo gets so worried about it.'

'I'm not surprised!'

'Tell me honestly, do you think I'm going out of my mind?'

'I very much doubt it. There are a lot of famous psychics, I believe, who are fully in possession of their faculties. In fact, the point seems to be that they have a few extra. Tell me about your trips to the past.'

As matter-of-factly as possible I related the transposition to the seashore below Orrisdale and my unwilling presence at the execution of William Christian. 'And yesterday, with Ray, it happened again to a lesser extent, both at Tynwald and Slieu Whallian. I think he was responsible for those, though, as a kind of test.'

There was a long silence, broken only by the rushing of the water tumbling down the valley in front of us and the calling of the inevitable gulls that wheeled overhead. As they had wheeled when Illiam Dhone's blood soaked

111

into the white blankets, and long years before that, when the Vikings gathered on Tynwald Hill. Somehow, I knew, my destiny was woven into the fabric of this little island as surely as theirs had been.

'About Ray,' Neil said abruptly, breaking into my musings. 'He shouldn't be allowed to get away with it. It's positively—Machiavellian. The obvious solution would be to contact his uncle again and let him—disconnect you.'

'He couldn't the last time.'

'But perhaps if you were conscious, and actively trying to free yourself—'

'Ray would never tell me where he is. He doesn't want the connection broken.'

'Knowing Ray,' Neil said dryly, 'I can't help suspecting that it isn't only your mind he's interested in!'

I smiled slightly. 'He doesn't have it all his own way, whatever he was saying at the inn. Now that I realize what he's doing I can sometimes block him off.'

'I'm relieved to hear it. And you reckon the dreams you have are also due to the hypnotist?'

'It seems likely. He knows all about Manx history and folklore.'

'If you want my opinion, I think you should pack your bags and fly home immediately. It all strikes me as decidedly unhealthy. I'm sure someone would be able to trace the man for you.'

'But if Ray brought me here this time, he could do it again.'

'Oh come now, Chloe! Assert yourself! You've a mind of your own, haven't you?'

'I'm not sure,' I said carefully.

He put a hand over mine. 'I'm sorry—an unfortunate choice of words! Seriously, though, I should put the greatest possible distance between you and Ray at the earliest opportunity. And loth though I am to worry Hugo, it's more than time that he was put fully in the picture. For one thing I don't care for the sole responsibility of knowing what you've told me.'

'You don't have to feel responsible for me,' I said bleakly. His repeated insistence on my going home was not at all what I wanted to hear.

'But good heavens, girl, of course I do! Would you expect me to stand by and look the other way while he turns you into some grotesque kind of puppet?'

'I shouldn't have told you. I'm sorry.' I was perilously close to tears but I'd no intention of letting him know.

'Well, you have, and Lord knows it's given me plenty to think about. I know the power of the mind is only just beginning to be fully appreciated but this! Ye gods, we've got premonition, time-hopping, telepathy and retrocognition, all in one bewildered girl! What worries me is how long you can hold

113

your head above water.'

Over to our left purple storm clouds were massing and their giant shadows went racing down the hillsides, momentarily blotting out the colours. Neil stood up. 'And talking of water we'd better be making a move or we'll be caught in the rain. It's slippery enough down there as it is. I'll go first and catch you if you fall!'

Down among the crowding trees it was suddenly much darker and cooler. The handrail alongside the first flight of steps soon gave out and the steep path plunged into the dimness, unfenced and potentially dangerous.

'All right?' Neil called back.

'So far.' I slithered after him, the noise of the waterfall roaring in my ears. On one side of the path dank gleaming rock dripped mournfully and the thin grey tree trunks were marred with the green leprosy of lichen.

'Watch this bit—it's lethal.' He reached back a hand and I clung to it as I started down the muddy slope. For a while the descent took all our concentration and we went in silence, but as it eased off slightly he said over his shoulder, 'These dreams of yours, are they all in the past?'

'No. There's one particularly horrible one where I'm lost in the mist on a hill somewhere.' I put my hand against the rock face to steady myself and gasped as my fingers sank into spongy green moss. 'Actually, I've had that one several times, beginning with a fairly mild, condensed version and gradually building up to the full horror.'

Down here at the foot of the gorge the trees were deciduous, their bare arms lifting in supplication to the distant sky while a few yellow leaves clung sparsely to the lower branches. I was thankful I hadn't attempted this walk alone. Hugo couldn't have realized the extent to which the recent heavy rains had intensified the dangers of the path, turning some of the steeper parts into a treacherous slide. We came to a wooden bridge and paused for a moment to look back upstream at the thundering descent of the waterfall.

'It's probably none of my business,' Neil said suddenly, 'but do please be careful with Ray. The more I think about what you told me, the less I like it. Whether or not he really has any hold over you, the fact that he thinks he has could be enough.'

I gazed down into the water frothing below the bridge. 'It's not only Ray, though. I've a feeling that the island and I have been waiting for each other for some time.'

'Which comment certainly doesn't make me feel any better! I must say you're the most intriguing girl; with all your dreams and portents. This afternoon has been quite a revelation. Just—take care of yourself, that's all.' He hesitated a moment and then pulled me gently towards him. His mouth was warm

115

and firm, intensely familiar and well-remembered. It was over in a minute and I had to make a conscious effort not to pull him closer and make the embrace altogether more important than he'd intended.

'Will you have dinner with me one evening?' His voice was studiedly casual.

'Thank you, I'd like to.'

'There's a staff meeting one evening this week. I'll have to check and give you a ring.' In the five minutes we had been on the bridge it had become noticeably darker. 'We'd better go, or Hugo will think the bugganes have got you!'

He took my hand and we went in silence along the dark, narrow path until, abruptly, it ended and the wooden building of the inn came into sight, with Neil's car parked next to Martha's in front of it. The glen was darkening rapidly now, premature evening shadows hastened by the storm clouds which were still marshalling on the hills. We stopped by the cars and looked at each other a little awkwardly. Then Neil smiled his slow, crooked smile and held my hand for a moment between both of his.

'Off you go then, and don't forget to tell Hugo about all this. I'll phone when I've checked about the meeting.'

He stood waiting while I started the car and moved slowly out on to the road. In the mirror I could see him still standing looking after me until I came to the bend and turned out of his sight.

CHAPTER TEN

Annette St Cyr had rung while I was out to let me know that she was well enough to return to work, and I was surprised when, the next morning, Martha called that she was on the phone again.

'Gaston and I were wondering if you've time to come over for a quick coffee this morning? We'd love to meet you, and thank you personally for helping out as you did. I have to leave for college about eleven, but if you could be here around ten o'clock it would give us an hour or so.'

The storm clouds which had gathered over Tholt-y-Will were falling as heavy rain when, an hour later, I drew up in the little car-park alongside the restaurant. Annette St Cyr opened the door as I reached it. She was tall, with wide grey eyes and dark hair tied back in a businesslike ponytail.

'Welcome to the Viking!'

I looked about me with interest. The room in which we stood was long and fairly narrow, its stone walls colour-washed in a warm shade of cream, and the heavy beams and rafters were a reminder of its days as a coach-house.

Ten or twelve tables lined the walls, most of them only large enough for two, and at the far end of the room, alongside an enormous open fireplace, an impressive array of hotplates introduced a note of modern efficiency. Over the fireplace hung a model of a Viking longboat.

'It doesn't look its best at ten o'clock on a wet Monday morning,' Annette remarked with a smile, 'but when the tables are laid and the lamps lit it really has quite an atmosphere.'

'I'm sure it has. And you run it entirely by yourselves?'

'Except for Nancy Finn from the village who comes in to do the washing-up. It's pretty hard work, I can tell you. Come through to the kitchen and meet Gaston.'

Gaston St Cyr was slightly shorter than his wife, as typical a Frenchman as one could imagine, with huge spaniel-like eyes and dropping moustaches. I automatically greeted him in French, to Annette's obvious approval.

'Is this tonight's menu?' I asked with interest, picking up the heavy card from the kitchen table.

'*Mais oui.*' Gaston looked over my shoulder. 'You will see, *mademoiselle* that we specialize in *cuisine bourgeoise* rather than *haute cuisine*. There are different *plats regionaux* each evening—*cassoulet, fruits de mer* and so on, and there is always offered also one English dish—baked ham or a roast of some sort.' He

118

spoke with a strong Provençal accent, reminding me forcibly of Jean-Claude at the hotel in the mountains.

Annette was pouring boiling water into the coffee jug. 'We hadn't realized you were a professional cook yourself until your brother mentioned it on the phone. I hope you didn't show me up too much! I'm very much the assistant round here, doing the roasts and vegetables and things that aren't too complicated.' She picked up the jug. 'Let's go upstairs.'

The stairway to the flat above led from the little passageway behind the kitchen where I had collected my supplies the previous week, emerging directly into a small living-room, plainly and comfortably furnished. A tray of French pottery coffee cups was laid ready on the table before the fire.

'I'd better confess,' Annette added as we sat down, 'that we asked you here with an ulterior motive.'

'Oh?'

'Your brother was saying you hadn't decided what you want to do.'

Excitement moved inside me. 'That's right.'

'We've been looking for someone to join us for some time; not just an employee—to be honest, we couldn't afford to pay out any wages—but someone who really knows about cookery and is prepared to put some money into the business—come in as a partner. As I said, my contribution is limited and Gaston really needs more experienced help.'

Gaston was gauging my reaction. 'And you, *mademoiselle*. It is essential that you go to London?'

'Not essential, no.'

'Then might our proposal be of interest? We should be happy to discuss it in greater detail if the idea appeals to you.'

I said slowly, 'It's very kind of you both.'

'*Au contraire, mademoiselle*, it is very much in our own interests. As my wife tells you, we have felt this need for some time but it is not easy to find someone who, as well as being of the standard we require, is also—how shall I say?—*sympathique*.'

I sipped my coffee, analysing this new opening. The challenge of helping to run the restaurant, doing exactly what I most enjoyed, was exciting enough. Added to that—and in my heart I knew this was even more important to me—it would offer the chance of staying within reach of Neil. 'I'll have to talk it over with my brother, of course.'

'*Bien sûr*. It is not a decision one can arrive at without consideration. We shall not attempt to hurry you.'

We talked then more generally of France and its regions. I learned that Gaston had been brought up in the catering business: his parents ran a small restaurant in Aix-en-Provence. I told him about the hotel where I had worked during the summer and he remembered the new management taking over.

At eleven o'clock Annette began to collect the coffee cups together. 'You two go on talking, but if you'll excuse me I'll have to be on my way.'

Feeling that her husband was anxious now to return to the kitchen, I made my excuses and left with her.

'I do hope you'll decide to join us,' she said as we went down the stairs together. 'It would be the answer to a prayer. Gaston has far too much to do at the moment.'

'And I suppose you'll have to start taking things more easily now.'

She looked at me quickly. 'How do you mean?'

'Well, with the baby—' I broke off at the look on her face.

'How did you know about that?'

'I'm sorry, I—didn't you say—?'

'No, I didn't! I'm not sure yet myself—I haven't even mentioned it to Gaston!'

'I'm very sorry,' I said again from a dry mouth. 'I can't imagine what put the idea in my head.' But I could.

'It doesn't matter, though I'd be grateful if you'd keep your suspicions to yourself for the moment. But you're right, of course. If I am pregnant, my days of working all hours of the day are numbered, though any baby of ours

121

will have to get used to spending its time in the kitchen! Anyway, talk it all over with your brother and let us know what you decide. We'll be keeping out fingers crossed.'

'Will you come back to the life class this afternoon?' Martha asked as we finished our lunch. 'The boys really ought to have another go at last week's sketches.'

'Not today, if you don't mind. If the weather improves I'll probably have to sit for Ray all day tomorrow and there are several letters I must write this afternoon.'

The telephone rang as Martha was fastening her mack. 'I can't stop now, I'm late as it is. If it's for me, say I'll ring back.'

But it was Neil, for me. 'I've just been checking through my diary. The meeting I mentioned is tomorrow, unfortunately, so our dinner date will have to wait till Wednesday, if that suits you. Is there anywhere you'd particularly like to go?'

'I've heard the Viking is very good.' And it would be interesting to judge it from the other side of the table as it were.

'Right, I'll phone and book a table. I missed you at lunch time, by the way. The mashed potatoes lacked your special touch!'

Smilingly I put down the phone, but as I was turning away a sudden sharp pain in my hand made me cry out involuntarily. I wasn't aware of having knocked it, and when I examined it I could see no sign of any cut, though the base of my left thumb was very tender to my probing fingers. Shrugging it aside, I went in search of writing-paper.

For a while I wrote steadily: a formal little note to my parents, a more informative account of the holiday to a girl friend, and several pages in French to Jean-Claude. I wondered if he was still hoping I'd go back to France for Christmas as he'd suggested. That was another possible outlet for my culinary skills—*La Patronne* at *Les Cinq Nids*. The fact that never once had it occurred to me to stay there was indication enough that my interest in Jean-Claude had never been, and I knew now never would be, serious. So I wrote lightly and non-committally about my plans, and hoped he would realize that my decision had in fact been reached before we even parted.

I was addressing the last envelope when the door bell rang and I opened it to find Vivian Quayle under a huge umbrella.

'My dear, I hope this isn't an inconvenient time to call?'

'Not at all, but I'm afraid Martha's at college this afternoon.'

'Actually it was you I wanted to see. I have a favour to ask.'

'Oh?' I quickly masked my surprise. 'Come in, then. Would you like a cup of tea? I was just about to make one.'

'That would be lovely.'

She shook the surplus rain from her

umbrella, leant it against the wall of the porch and stepped into the hall. I took her coat and left her in the sitting-room while I hurried to put on the kettle. My left hand was throbbing painfully, though there was still nothing visible to account for the discomfort. When I returned with the tray, Vivian was standing at the window looking out at the wet, misty countryside.

'How depressing everything seems in the rain, all sodden and water-logged. I know there's usually a magnificent view from this window.' She smiled slightly. 'Give the island its due, the scenery is superb.'

I poured the tea and handed over her cup and saucer. 'What was it you wanted to ask me?'

'I don't know if Martha has mentioned it, but the village branch of the Women's Institute is holding its annual bazaar on Thursday and I've just had a phone call to say Mrs Pargiter, who runs the cake stall, is ill and won't be able to help this year. It's an awful blow at such short notice. She's the backbone of the committee and as well as running the stall, usually supplies over half the goods herself.' She looked at me appealingly over the rim of her cup. 'I imagine you've guessed what I want to ask.'

'I'll make some cakes for you, certainly.'

'Would you, my dear? I'd be so grateful. And could you also take over the stall? It's not

124

too arduous really and would be such a load off my mind.'

'I should think so. How many cakes will you need?'

'As many as you can manage! They'll all go. And if you'd be a love and produce one really special *gâteau*, we could raffle it. There are about a dozen stalls altogether, fancy goods, stationery, indoor plants—you know the kind of thing. It's largely run by college wives, of course, since St Olaf's accounts for at least two-thirds of the population of Ballacarrick. Have you met any of them?'

'One or two, at the King Orry last week. They seemed very pleasant.'

'Oh, they're all right in small doses, I suppose. The trouble is there's no getting away from them. We have a very narrow social circle, as you can imagine. The same faces show up everywhere—church, bridge, the W.I., not to mention these infernal sherry parties we have hanging over our heads each term. And of course gossip is rife; Ray Kittering sees to that.' Her eyes flicked in my direction. 'I hear he's fastened on to you, my dear. Do for pity's sake be careful and watch what you say. He has an unpleasant knack of twisting your words and throwing them back at you. Believe me, I should know. He had the impudence to make a pass at me once. I soon put him in his place and he's never forgiven me.'

She leant back in her chair and lit a

cigarette. 'Everyone knows everyone's business—it's inevitable. That's why it was so humiliating when Frank Harrison stepped in front of Nicholas and took over as deputy. The whole of St Olaf's knew Nicholas came over on the specific understanding that the post should be his. Of course, the headmaster's a fool.' She exhaled, watching the smoke spiral towards the ceiling. 'A well-meaning, jovial fool, far too easily influenced. It never occurred to Nicholas to kow-tow to him but Frank Harrison had no such scruples and look where it got him. It's amazing what a bit of buttering up can accomplish and our worthy head is as susceptible to flattery as the next man.' She gave a brittle little laugh. 'He's known throughout college as H.M., you know. I remember Simon Fenton saying once he was sure the old boy thought it stood for His Majesty!'

Her eyes came back to my face. 'You must think it's all very parochial and childish, this jostling for position and caring what everyone thinks of you. Believe me, so did I at first, but somehow you get sucked into the stream yourself. I honestly don't know how I'd have held on these last few years if it hadn't been for Neil.'

'Old Vivian has quite a hankering for him,' said the serpent's voice in my ear. Almost as though she'd read my mind she smiled wryly.

'No doubt friend Ray had Neil and me

tucked up in bed together long since. In his world there's no such thing as platonic friendship.'

I moved to the fire to screen my burning cheeks and threw on another log. I was realizing for the first time that Ray's poison was so insidious that I'd been in danger of half-believing it and I was bitterly ashamed.

'God!' Vivian burst out explosively, 'if only Nicholas could land this Downhurst appointment! There might still be time for him to make his mark after all. He's brilliant, you know, completely wasted in a backwater like this.'

She bent forward and put down her cup and saucer. 'But I'm boring you again. It's an occupational hazard, my dear. Forgive me. And I've taken up quite enough of your time. Thanks so much for agreeing to help us out. The bazaar is held in St Stephen's Hall, by the way. It opens at three, so if you could be there by two it would give us time to get everything out and price it. And you might remind Martha, she's on fancy goods this year. She did say she'd contribute a shawl or something, but ten to one she's forgotten all about it!'

As I watched Vivian go down the drive under the giant mushroom of her umbrella I was planning what I should bake for the stall. Perhaps Annette would lend me a few recipes.

Martha returned from her class soon afterwards. 'You were right about Pam's phone call,' she said expressionlessly, dropping a bundle of sketches on to the coffee table.

'Oh?' I closed my eyes briefly against a wave of sickness.

'Phyl Lathom told me at break. Apparently she did go to the King Orry, but she was obviously uneasy, Phyl said, and left early. She'd just got back when it came through.'

I said with an effort, 'Who was it, do you know?'

'Her sister, in Douglas. She'd taken an overdose of sleeping-pills after a row with her boy-friend. Then she panicked and phoned Pam. She passed out during the call but they were able to rush an ambulance to her in time. If Pam hadn't been in, though—'

She broke off and after a long silence I said tonelessly, 'That's all right, then.'

Martha glanced across at me. 'Don't expect any thanks,' she said dryly. 'Pam's insisting it's all coincidence.'

A regular little sybil, she had called me. Being proved right was unlikely to endear me to her any further. I pushed the incident out of my head and tried to concentrate on the Viking.

Over dinner that evening I said to Hugo, 'Did Martha tell you I had coffee at the Viking this morning?'

'I think she mentioned it, yes. They're a pleasant couple, aren't they?'

'Very. As a matter of fact, they've asked me

if I'd like to go in with them.'

'Chloe! You never told me!' Martha stared at me round-eyed.

'Sorry, but there seemed no point in going through it twice.'

'Permanently, you mean?' Hugo demanded.

'More or less.'

'And how do you feel about it?'

'It's just the sort of place I'd love to have. I don't know what kind of profit they make, how it balances out throughout the year and so on, but we could soon find out if I decide to go ahead. What do you think?'

'My dear girl, only you can decide. I thought you'd set your sights on London, though?'

'The competition would be pretty stiff and you know what a coward I am. I've been dreading the thought of having to break into a profession with no-one near I could run to for help.'

'Oh, nonsense. You set out for France on your own without a backward glance.'

'That wasn't bravery; I was in full retreat from Oxford.'

'Well, from our angle, of course, we'd be delighted if you stayed.'

'But?' I prompted shrewdly.

'It's just struck me that you'd be subjected to an indefinite proximity to Ray. I can't say I'm too happy about that.'

'He always said I'd stay, didn't he?'

Hugo looked at me with narrowed eyes. 'I

trust that didn't have any influence on you.'

'No, of course not.' I added quickly and with deliberate lightness: 'Anyway, he's not the only man in my life! I'm having dinner with Neil on Wednesday.'

To my surprise, the remark was greeted with total silence. Then Martha said softly, 'Oh Hugo, I did tell you—'

I looked sharply from one to the other. 'What's the matter? Is something wrong?'

'No, of course not.' Hugo's fingers crumbled the bread on his plate. 'It's only—well, I shouldn't count too much on Neil, love. There's Pam in the offing, and—'

'I'm not *counting* on him at all,' I retorted, 'but after all it is the second time he's asked me out, so—' I broke off at their exchanged glances. 'Hugo, will you please tell me what's going on?'

'Tell her,' Martha urged. She didn't meet my eyes.

Hugo said awkwardly, 'Of course, I didn't think you'd be here longer than a couple of weeks or so, but—'

'Go on,' I said tightly.

'Well, as you know I didn't care for the effect Ray seemed to have on you, so I—well, I hinted vaguely to Neil that I'd feel a lot easier if he could step in—as a kind of counterbalance.'

I could hear my heartbeats crashing round my head. I kept my eyes on Hugo's averted, embarrassed face. 'You mean,' I said clearly, 'you asked him to take me out a couple of times to divert my attention from Ray? Strictly no strings, of course—after all, I was only here for two weeks—that kind of thing?'

'Not in so many words, naturally, but I imagine he knew what I was getting at. There didn't seem any harm in it. Damn it, there wouldn't have been if—'

'If I'd gone home like a good girl when I should have done. Well!' I drew a deep breath. 'It seems I've been overestimating my powers of attraction!'

'Oh Chloe, love, don't take it like that! Neil likes you, after all. The idea wouldn't have occurred to me if I hadn't noticed that. I'm sure it was no hardship for him to—'

'Oblige?' I cut in viciously. 'I must say he quite entered into the spirit of the thing. He even kissed me yesterday.' I scraped back my chair but Martha caught my arm.

'Can't we talk this over more calmly? I did try to tell Hugo it wasn't an awfully good idea but he was so anxious about you and Ray. And knowing him he'd have been so diffident about it, it's quite possible Neil never even realized what he was trying to say.' As I still didn't reply her fingers tightened on my arm and she gave it a little shake. 'Chloe, don't let this weigh with your plans. You'll have to try to put both Neil and Ray out of your head if you're going to be businesslike about the Viking. Suppose neither of them was within a hundred miles of it. Would you still be interested in taking it on?'

'Yes,' I said after a minute.

'Right, then it seems worth looking into further. It's your career you're considering, after all, not a couple of dinner dates.'

If only it had been as simple as that.

I turned to Hugo. 'You'd better release Neil from his commitment, then,' I said levelly, 'and never, never do anything like that again.'

'I'm sorry,' he said quietly. 'Believe me, if I'd realized—'

'And of course if I do decide to stay I'll be looking round for a place of my own, so let me know if you hear of anywhere suitable.'

'You know you're welcome here for as long as you want to stay.' He smiled slightly. 'I haven't had indigestion once since you arrived!'

'Will you come with me to speak to the St Cyrs?'

'Of course. We'll need to know how much they'd like you to invest and what kind of a return you can expect. I think it might be wise to build in some kind of time clause, too, in case you find it's not what you want after all. You could agree to renew the partnership in, say, two years if both sides are agreeable.'

'I'll phone them and fix a time to go round. I want to borrow some recipe books as well. Vivian Quayle called this afternoon and persuaded me to take over the cake stall at the bazaar on Thursday.'

'Oh Lord!' Martha exclaimed. 'I'd forgotten about that! I still haven't finished the shawl I'm knitting for it.'

'Don't commit yourself too far until we've sounded them out thoroughly,' Hugo called after me as I hurried to the phone. This, I told myself as I dialled with unsteady fingers, was what I must fasten my mind on. For the moment I didn't trust myself to think of Neil, nor dare to think of Ray. As Martha had reminded me, my career was—must be—the most important thing to decide.

CHAPTER ELEVEN

I was not looking forward to my sitting with Ray and found myself regretting the challenge I had so recklessly issued. Whether it was he or the unwitting Tom Kelly who had subjected me to the terrors of Slieu Whallian, I suspected that the more I saw of him, the more readily would those indeterminate barriers go down and I should slip with increasing ease into other dimensions.

To add to my wretchedness my pride was urging me to cancel the dinner date with Neil. The probability that I owed it to Hugo still rankled but the fact remained that with a concentrated day of Ray ahead I needed the thought of Neil to steady me, even if our evening together would be a contrived arrangement.

When Ray called for me I saw at once that there was a bandage on his hand and felt a stab of fear before I realized why. 'What have you done to your hand?'

'Nothing serious, it's just a nuisance. My penknife slipped and there's quite a deep gash round the base of the thumb. Matron insisted I went for an anti-tetanus jab.'

My own hand throbbed briefly, stopping as my will-power clamped down on it. I said on a high note, 'I wasn't sure what you wanted me to wear.'

'I brought some things with me.' He handed over a large paper bag. 'I hope they fit.'

I opened the bag and drew out a long woollen skirt and matching stole in soft blue and green plaid. 'Ray, they're lovely! Whose are they?'

'My sister's. She doesn't mind. Go and try them on. That white blouse you wore the other day should go with them.'

In my bedroom I changed hurriedly and found that the plaid skirt fitted to perfection. I draped the stole round my shoulders and turned to survey my reflection in the full-length mirror. There was no denying that the ensemble was very flattering and my pleasure in it helped to smooth away at least some of the constraint between us.

Ray gave a sigh of satisfaction. 'Perfect. It's the Manx tartan, you see; traditionally made up of the blue of the sky, the green of the hills, the purple of the heather and the gold of the gorse. Sure now, it could have been designed for you.'

The sun was shining as we drove out of the lane and turned left for Ballaugh. Outside the school gates the stuffed guy, his face hidden by the wide-brimmed hat, lolled grotesquely in his barrow.

'Poor Guy Fawkes, what a death sentence!' I said lightly. 'To be burned every fifth of November till the end of time!'

'I've always felt sorry for him myself, but then it wasn't my parliament he tried to blow up. I suppose the "come-overs" from the mainland brought the custom with them at some stage. Hallows' E'en isn't imported, though. Witches are part of our own history, as you found out yourself.'

Beneath his casual tone lay a deliberate reminder of his power over me and of the challenge given and accepted. It served as a timely warning that however innocuous our companionship might seem I would be wise not to lower my guard.

We followed the road for some five or six miles before Ray turned off and circled round the base of a small hill, 'That's where we're aiming for,' he told me, indicating the summit with a jerk of his head. 'It's easy enough going up this side but there's a very steep climb on the other. Can you manage the picnic basket if I take the painting equipment? I've to be careful not to strain this blasted thumb.'

As we started the climb I saw that Ray's assessment of 'easy going' was not the same as mine. It was a full ten minutes before we were on level ground, but as I stopped to get my breath back I saw that it had been well worthwhile. Up here we were surrounded by grey rock, dried heather and turf, a scene surely unchanged over thousands of years, while beyond lay the coastline, majestic and awe-inspiring with its towering cliffs, its white shingle and the depth of blue which stretched unbroken to the Irish coast.

'I wanted it all, you see,' Ray said, watching as I took in the panorama, 'hills, sea, gorse and heather—and you in your Manx tartan. The composite picture. Have a look round while I set everything up.'

I went cautiously over the uneven ground, picking my way round wind-bent bushes and outcrops of rock. He was right about the steep drop on this far side. The road seemed a surprisingly long way down. Here the salt wind blew full in my face and the gulls, screaming discordantly, were tossed up in the currents of air like scraps of white paper.

Something about the timeless majesty of the surroundings triggered in my imagination a misty awareness of those who over the centuries had stood here before me: Vikings, keeping watch and ward, Celts, Scots, all of them leaving some indefinable imprint on this exposed jut of land as, perhaps, would I.

'Ready when you are!' Ray called and I turned from my brooding and went back to him. He had set up one of the small stools by a clump of gorse, browning now but still with a touch of gold in its depths.

'I want you in semi-profile,' he told me, 'staring out to sea. Yes, I know the wind's blowing your hair. That's the way I want it.'

I settled myself on the stool and he arranged the folds of skirt and stole to his satisfaction, moving my head with a finger beneath my chin. 'That's fine. Now keep as still as you can and we'll break for coffee in an hour or so.'

For a while I sat motionless looking out across the short scrubby grass to the cliff edge, etched clear as a pencil line against the blue of the sky. The wind rustled in the drying gorse behind me and I was grateful for the soft warmth of the stole. Out of the corner of my eye I could see the movement of Ray's arm as he sketched in the preliminary lines of the portrait. It was very peaceful.

'Are you going to the famous sherry party on Friday?' he asked after a while. 'No, don't move your head! Martha and Hugo won't be able to get out of it; there's one a term and

137

attendance is more or less compulsory. Supposed to give us all a chance to meet socially, if you please, as if we don't see enough of each other as it is! Still, I usually manage to amuse myself by watching people's reactions to each other. It's amazing how they can say one thing with their mouths and something entirely different with their eyes or a movement of their heads. You can learn a lot if you know what to look for, and them never guessing they've given themselves away.'

'And you can also misinterpret a lot,' I put in severely, remembering his remarks about Neil and Vivian.

'Not I, my love. I can gauge these things to the nth degree—relationships that are brewing and others about to break up. Take Sheila Shoesmith and young David, for instance. I shouldn't give them more than a couple of weeks. How they've managed to keep it from Martin this long I'll never know. They've been making good use of the sports pavilion the whole of this term. Do you know them, by the way?'

'I've met Sheila,' I said stiffly, 'but—'

'David's the games master, which you must admit is appropriate! More brawn than brain, of course, but at least he's bright enough to play two dolly-birds at the same time—he's got our delectable *mademoiselle* eating out of his hand as well. You know Claudine? Now there's a girl not afraid to toss her bonnet over the windmill! Wouldn't the fur be flying if Sheila found out? Sure, I might drop the odd hint and stand back to see what happens!'

'I don't want to hear any more,' I interrupted. 'You know, I'd hate to see the world through your eyes, Ray. You make it all so—shabby.'

'But interesting, Chloe my love, interesting! It would be a dull world if we were all strait-laced, now wouldn't it? And you can take that disapproving look off your face, for if I paint it in it will spoil the picture entirely!'

He lapsed into silence and I could only be thankful. My neck was beginning to feel stiff and there was a stabbing pain between my shoulder blades. Before my fixed gaze the purple horizon shimmered and danced.

'O.K.,' Ray said at last. 'Five-minute break. There's coffee in the flask.'

I stood thankfully, rubbing my stiff back.

'Warm enough?'

'So-so. The coffee will help.' I clasped my hands round the hot mug and walked over to the easel. The figure that was myself was still vague, a mere outline set against its background, yet the contours of the face were recognizable as my own. I stood looking at it while I drank the coffee in cautious sips and Ray, sprawled on the grass, watched me in silence.

'Right,' he said abruptly, getting to his feet. 'Break over. Back to work.'

'I have the impression,' he remarked, breaking a silence of some fifteen minutes, 'that your worthy brother doesn't entirely approve of our association.'

'Can you blame him?' I asked acidly.

He looked up. 'He knows? About the connection we have?'

'No, actually he doesn't yet, but I gather your reputation with women isn't all that it might be.'

He smiled sourly. 'Telepathy has its uses.'

A coldness caressed my neck under the fall of hair. 'What's that supposed to mean?'

'Well now, my love, you might not have noticed but I'm not the most popular character around here. Wouldn't win any prizes for the "chap most likely" or anything like that. So it's extraordinarily useful to be able to persuade the odd delectable bird that she's simply dying to jump into bed with me. It's surprising how often it works.'

I turned to stare at him in incredulous horror. 'You really do that?'

'Why not? I'd go a bit short if I didn't.'

My mind swung dizzily to our first meeting and the tumult of sensations that had whirled inside me. Later I had even wondered whether—

'You tried it on me, didn't you?' Accusation rang in my voice.

'You weren't as susceptible as the others, though. Surprising, when I can usually get

140

straight through to you. Not that I'm complaining, mind. It might take longer but I'm enjoying the struggle, and there's no doubt you'll come round in the end. Wasn't that why I brought you here?'

I couldn't believe he was serious, but all the same it seemed time to put the record straight. 'Ray, I might as well tell you—'

'You're wasting your time with Neil Sheppard, you know. Vivian's got him all neatly sewn up, and Pam conveniently acts as a blind. Suits him admirably, I shouldn't wonder—all the perks and none of the responsibilities.'

I stood up abruptly. 'I refuse to be your captive audience while you let your disgusting imagination run riot. I'm not listening to any more.'

'Well now, I touched a sensitive spot there, didn't I?' He looked up at me. 'Sit down, little Chloe. I'm trying to paint you, remember.'

I stood glaring back at him but my threat was an empty one. I should merely look foolish if I flounced down the hill and had to stand waiting by his car until he chose to come after me. Rebelliously I sat down again.

'We'd better get this clear,' I said shakily after a minute. 'Once and for all, there will never be anything between us other than this mental hook-up. It's important that you accept this because I might be staying on after all.'

'I knew it all along. Didn't I tell you, and

141

you so stubborn about it? You'll probably end by staying even longer than I do.'

I turned sharply, forgetting my pose, and met his raised eyebrows. 'And what have I said now?'

It wasn't rational, but with spreading coldness I knew the reason for my instinctive alarm. I should indeed be here longer than Ray, because his days were already numbered. Underlining my icy premonition the sun slid suddenly behind a bank of cloud. 'I'm cold,' I said sharply.

He put down his brush. 'We'll have lunch, then, and give the sun a chance to come through again.'

In silence we unpacked the hamper and Ray spread a groundsheet on the still-damp grass.

'Remember me telling you about Granny Clegg? I'll take you down to see her when we've finished here. She's a weird old body but she knows all the island stories. She'll make your hair stand on end with her tales of the foawr and the lhiannan-shee.'

My hand brushed against his as I laid out the sandwiches and I felt him tense. 'I'm glad you're staying, Chloe. You'll find I'm right about the other thing, too, so why not stop struggling like a good girl?' He reached for me and as I ducked away his expression changed. 'Has it not occurred to you that I don't need your permission? No-one's within miles of us here.'

I stared at him with suddenly pounding heart, noting the sweat on his upper lip and the little pulse beating at his temple.

'Ray, please—'

'Ray, please!' he mimicked savagely. 'Damn it, girl, have you no blood in your veins at all?' His arms came tightly round me, pinioning mine to my side and crushing the breath out of my body. Acute panic fused with the conflicting emotions that had been troubling me all morning into a brief, white-hot explosion and even as I tried to cry out, I knew that it was happening again. Perhaps this time it was a means of escape.

The cool October wind had fallen away and it was May, the old May Day before the change of the calendar. I was standing on the edge of a green field round which clustered a crowd of merrymakers, everyone decked out in garlands and chaplets of yellow flowers. The centre of the field was empty but as a horn sounded near at hand, two parties of young men advanced into it. To my surprise I saw that while one team was dressed in light open-necked shirts, the members of the other were wrapped closely in thick woollen coats and scarves and wore garlands of holly and ivy. It seemed that a mock battle was taking place, though I could not understand why, and for the first time during these switches I was aware of my own identity, of not belonging. I turned from the field to lay a hand urgently on the

143

arm of the man beside me.

'Please help me!' I began, 'I shouldn't be here!' And recoiled in horror as my hand went straight through his arm. Was he a ghost, then? Or, in this time band, was I? Certainly he hadn't even turned his head to look at me.

I stumbled away, swerving out of the path of the crowd and shutting my mind to the knowledge that I could if I wished go straight through them. And now they had started to sing and the insistent beat, the compulsory words branded themselves on my brain so that I found myself singing with them:

'Robin-y-Ree! Robin-y-Ree! Ridlan aboo
abban fal dy ridlan, Robin-y-Ree!'

The green grass of the meadow came rushing up to meet me and I felt the hardness of it against my face and heard Ray's voice, sharp with fear. 'Chloe! Chloe, for God's sake what happened?'

I forced my eyes open to find myself lying amid the wreckage of the picnic lunch while Ray, kneeling beside me, was rubbing my hands between his own and the roughness of the bandage scratched my skin. Behind the fear in his eyes was a feverish excitement.

'What happened?' he demanded again. 'What was it you were saying, can you remember?'

The memory was becoming blurred and my tongue stumbled over the unfamiliar words. ' "Abban fal dy ridlan, Robin-y-Ree!" '

He drew a deep breath and sat back. 'Tell me everything!' he commanded, and I had no will to withstand him. Mechanically I described the field and the crowds while his eyes remained fixed almost hypnotically on my face. At last, because the words ran out, I stumbled to a halt.

'What was it?' I asked after a moment.

His voice shook with excitement. 'It seems to have been one of the old traditions, the battle of Summer and Winter. The chorus of that song, "Topknots of scarlet and ribbons of green"—hell, Chloe, you must actually have been *there*! How else—unless Uncle Tom—but even so, the power that would have been needed—'

Dizzily I sat up, a hand to my head.

'Has it happened before? Anything like this?' And again, as I hesitated, the imperious 'Tell me!' So I told him, about Illiam Dhone and then about the strange, snake-like dance on the hard sand near Kirk Michael.

'The Flitterdaunsey,' he muttered almost to himself. 'I remember Uncle telling me about it. It used to be held on Good Friday, when people went to the shore to gather flitters— limpets. Iron and steel couldn't be used on Good Friday so the barley bread was moulded by hand, and after the picnic any remaining food was thrown into the sea with the words—' He stopped, his eyes burning into me.

'"*Gow show as bannee orrin*"', I supplied

145

dully, though I wasn't aware of having heard the words before.

'That's right: "Take this and bless us". Chloe, why didn't you tell me all this before?'

'I was afraid,' I said in a low voice.

'Of what?'

Of admitting the extent of my involvement. I hadn't answered but I think he understood because he didn't press the point.

'Take me with you next time!' he said softly.

'How can I?' I burst out. 'If I'd any control at all over it I wouldn't let it happen!' I scrambled unsteadily to my feet. 'I don't want to talk about it any more. Please will you take me home?'

He rose to his feet. 'Very well, we'll go now, but not home. We're going to Granny Clegg's, remember. Perhaps she can tell us more about May Day and the Flitterdaunsey. Now—'as I started to protest—'go and see if you approve of the way your portrait's coming along.'

Obediently I walked over to look at the picture. Although the details were still vague the figure now had an almost uncanny resemblance to myself, with a depth about it that suggested he had been looking into as well as at me. I was reminded of the portrait of his grandmother, with its yearning sense of loneliness.

'Well?'

'It makes me a little uncomfortable.'

'Good. So it should. Now help me pack the

hamper, will you? This infernal bandage keeps getting in the way.'

We drove straight down the coast road to Peel and gradually, as Ray kept the conversation carefully inconsequential, my tension began to ease. The harbour was throbbing with boats of all descriptions and he pointed out Peel Island with the old ruined church of St German humped against the skyline. 'According to tradition St German was sent by St Patrick to found the Manx church. That would date it from the fifth century. And there's Peel Castle and Fenella's Tower. Walter Scott wrote about that.' He flashed me a glance. 'The castle's haunted, naturally, by the Moddy Dhoo, or Black Dog. If you see it, they say you'll die soon after.'

We drove slowly along the cobbled quayside and stopped in front of one of the old-time fishermen's cottages, whitewashed and snug now in the mellow sunshine.

'You'll have to shout,' Ray warned me. 'The Granny's as deaf as a post.'

His knock on the wooden door was answered by a tall angular woman in an apron. Her hair was scraped severely back and tied in a knot on top of her head, but her eyes, so deep a blue as to appear purple, were startlingly beautiful. They were oddly incongruous in such a setting, as though something lovely and fragile were imprisoned in the uncompromisingly awkward frame.

147

'Good day to you, Kirree. Would your mother be at home?'

'Isn't it yourself that knows she never crosses the threshold?'

'I've brought Miss Winter to see her, if it's convenient.'

The glorious eyes switched to me and I felt them lance into my brain. Then she nodded briefly and stood to one side. Ray motioned me ahead and we went in, bending our heads to avoid the low lintel. The one-roomed cottage had made little concession to the twentieth century. To my delight a spinning wheel stood in one corner, and a closer look at the skirt Kirree Clegg was wearing intimated that it was still very much in use. From the depths of a rocking-chair beside the turf fire, Granny surveyed us with beady black eyes. She was a tiny figure all in black, her grey hair screwed into the same style as her daughter's, her face seamed by myriads of wrinkles.

' 'Tis herself you've brought, then,' she greeted Ray, nodding vigorously. 'Didn't I tell you, daughter, when you dropped the knife at breakfast? Well now, child, I was expecting you.'

I moved to take the small claw she held out in my direction. 'Good afternoon, Mrs Clegg.'

The button-black eyes probed into mine. 'You've travelled far this day, I'm thinking.'

I said nothing, knowing that the distance she spoke of was measured not in miles but in

148

years.

' 'Tis temporary, this gift of yours, but not done yet. And there's trouble ahead.'

I winced and withdrew my hand from hers.

'Trouble, and danger in the mist.'

'Oh come on now, Granny, is that the way to greet a visitor, at all?'

'I tells what I sees,' the old woman insisted stubbornly. 'Sure and she's not a simpleton. Doesn't she know it herself already?' Her eyes slid past me to Ray and a glazed expression clouded them. 'Begun in September, done ere November,' she muttered indistinctly.

He gave a nervous laugh. 'Aren't you full of the croaks of doom today!'

'Evil comes home to roost, son, and don't say I wasn't after warning you.'

'Never mind me, now. Chloe wants to hear some of your fairy tales.' But the old woman had turned away to stare into the depths of the fire, shaking her head and rocking gently.

'You'll be getting no more out of her today,' Kirree said matter-of-factly. 'Will you stay for a cup of tea?'

But the old woman's words, mystifying though they were, had disturbed us both and after a quickly exchanged glance Ray shook his head. 'Not today, Kirree, thanks all the same. Since the Granny's not herself we won't bother you any longer.'

'It's welcome you'll be another time,' she said kindly, 'and Mother will read the lassie's

149

hand if the mood takes her right.'

'Thank you,' I said awkwardly. My eyes went back to the tiny rocking figure muttering to herself in the depths of the old chair. 'Good-bye, Mrs Clegg.'

There was no reply and after a brief exchange of formalities Ray and I were outside on the quay again. We had been in the cottage barely ten minutes. Unaccountably it seemed much longer.

Back in the car we drove in silence for some time, until I said suddenly, 'She didn't seem at all deaf.'

'She was hearing with her inner ear today. Clairaudience and clairvoyance often go together.' He paused. 'I wonder what that doggerel about September and November was supposed to mean.'

I'd wondered, too. And about the danger in the mist she had foreseen for me. The dream, perhaps.

'Has she ever told you anything that came true?' I asked uneasily.

'Nothing momentous. She'll say something like "There's a letter coming from across the sea" when I'd written to someone on the mainland and was expecting a reply anyway.'

'Has she read your hand?'

'Once or twice, over the years. Again, all very vague and ambiguous. "Beware the coloured stars"—that kind of thing, and she leaves you to unravel it as best you can. No, she's a bit of a dead loss when it comes to fortune-telling, but she's really great on legend. A pity she was in one of her more wafty moods today.'

The blueness of evening was settling over the countryside as we came up shadowed Glen Helen and by the time Ray finally drew up outside Hugo's cottage the stars were out.

'My timetable's full for the rest of the week, but you'll give me another sitting on Saturday, won't you?'

A tremor of unease inched up my spine. 'I don't know.'

'I'll have to behave myself, is that it?'

But that wasn't the only reason why I felt a strong reluctance to sit for Ray again.

He reached for my hand and, as I stiffened, said quickly, 'Relax, I'm not going to force myself on you. That's been my mistake all along, hasn't it? I'm used to having to fight for what I want but I should have realized it was different with you. You'll come to me in your own good time. I know that now.'

I said with difficulty, 'Ray, I tried to explain—'

He lifted my hand to his mouth and held it there while I sat like a rock staring at the shaggy bent head and feeling his lips move over the surface of my palm. And such was the strength of his will that, appalled, I began to wonder if he was right. I tugged my hand free and said breathlessly, 'You're wrong, quite

151

wrong. You must believe me.'

'No, my darling,' he said softly, 'you must believe me. I'm not one for making pretty speeches but we belong together, you and I. The fact that you came when I called you proves that. I'll wait if I have to; just don't let it be too long.'

I gazed at him speechlessly and he met my look with those deep, burning eyes unwavering on my face.

'Good-night,' I said in a rush, and almost fell out of the car. I had reached the front door before I heard him drive away.

Martha's exclamation on the tartan skirt and Hugo's deceptively casual enquiry about the sitting I dealt with as best I could. In the last ten minutes my relationship with Ray had changed out of all recognition, becoming at the same time deeper and more threatening. For despite my protestations he had felt sure enough of me to commit himself, and that was dangerous. I could only guess at his reaction to any imagined betrayal.

CHAPTER TWELVE

Annette had left some recipe books for me as requested and I was thankful that my contributions to the bazaar would occupy me for most of the day. As I'd anticipated,

Martha's store cupboard did not extend to such commodities as yeast, cream of tartar and ground almonds, and it was obvious that a trip to Ramsey would be my first priority.

The Ford's petrol gauge was almost on 'empty' so I turned into the first garage I came to and had pulled up at the pumps before I realized with a shock that the blue Renault already there belonged to Ray. Hastily I switched on the ignition again, but it was too late. He had come out of the office and caught sight of me, and I reluctantly got out of the car.

'You're out bright and early this morning!' he greeted me.

'So are you. Why aren't you at college?'

'I'm collecting an assortment of petrol tins for a still-life class. Where are you off to?'

'Ramsey. I've a lot of baking to do for the bazaar and need to stock up on supplies.'

'So you'll be spending the day slaving over a hot stove? Come out with me this evening to recuperate!'

'I'm sorry, I can't.'

'Why not?'

'I—already have an engagement.' I kept my eyes on the swiftly moving figures of the petrol pump.

'Have you now? Might I ask what it is?'

My finger nails were digging into my palms. Better this way, I told myself feverishly. He must be made to understand the position and

153

the sooner it was done the less damage might be inflicted.

'Well?' he asked with a touch of impatience. 'Is it a state secret?'

'No,' I answered as steadily as I could. 'As a matter of fact, I'm having dinner with Neil.'

He stared at me blankly. 'The hell you are! You kept pretty quiet about that yesterday.'

'It didn't seem relevant.'

'Oh, you think not? Well, it seems pretty damn relevant to me! What price all that coy "Don't touch me—I'm not that kind of girl!" when all the time—My God, you could teach Claudine Bouchet a trick or two, and that's saying something!'

'Ray, I did try to tell you—'

'And I'm willing to bet our Neil doesn't get fobbed off with any arm's length treatment! He's not one to waste his time if there's nothing in it for him—ask Pam or your precious Vivian! You rotten, two-faced little bitch! You even let me—' He broke off, fighting to control his breathing.

'Very well, my love, but you needn't think it changes the outcome one iota, just the way we go about it. If you want to play dirty, that's all right by me. In fact, I'll enjoy it. If Neil Sheppard knows what's good for him, he'll beat a hasty retreat back to Vivian's apron strings. Old Nicholas might turn a blind eye to a bit on the side, but by God I won't!'

The hunched shoulders of the garage

154

attendant registered avid if tactful interest. Without looking at him I held out a handful of notes, leaving him to extract the amount he required. Behind me Ray's car leapt forward with a roar, screeched across the forecourt and out on to the road. I was sorry for his first class that morning.

I stumbled into Martha's car and sat clutching the steering-wheel.

'Your change, Miss.' The man's voice was respectfully sympathetic.

'Thank you.' I took a deep breath and drove slowly out on to the road. That was one garage I shouldn't be able to use again.

The scene was still playing itself over and over in my head when I started on the baking later that morning.

'You're rather pale,' Martha remarked, hanging over me and watching my every move. 'Feeling all right?'

'Yes, thanks.' Mentally I resolved to leave the *gâteau* until she was at college and my attention would not be divided. In the meantime the cheese scones, crisp and golden, were cooling on the tray, the *petits fours* awaited decoration and the coffee cake was in the oven.

'I do envy you!' Martha sighed. 'You're so unflappable!'

I smiled with a touch of bitterness and did not reply.

Slowly, wrapped in an aroma of baking, the

long day passed. Martha went to her class after lunch and I made my *gâteau* methodically but without the enjoyment I'd anticipated. By five o'clock when Hugo returned the kitchen was spotless again.

'Lord, what a day!' He dropped into his easy chair. 'Martha, be a lamb and make me a cup of tea. I need reviving.' He glanced at me. 'Your friend Ray has been excelling himself today.'

'It was probably my fault,' I said quietly. 'We had rather an unpleasant confrontation at the garage this morning.'

'Perhaps that accounts for it. He was exceptionally foul, even for him. Had Pam Beecham in tears at break and there was a highly charged atmosphere every time he came into the staff-room, which to put it mildly was hardly conducive to the smooth running of the day. What happened, though? You seemed friendly enough yesterday.'

'I told him I was having dinner with Neil.'

'Ah! Well, let me repeat my warning, little sister. He can be a dangerous enemy. If I were you I should make a complete break as soon as possible. It was all right letting things ride when you were only here for a holiday, but if it's to be a permanent arrangement you certainly don't want to get embroiled with the likes of him.'

Nevertheless, embroiled was precisely what I was, and I knew despairingly that however much we may tug against it, the link between Ray and me would hold us together until something stronger than both of us severed it for good.

Neil called for me at seven-thirty. 'All right?' he asked, and the searching glance that accompanied the question made it more than rhetorical.

'Yes, thanks.'

'The table's booked for eight-thirty so we've time for a visit to the King Orry first.'

'I'm glad you could make it this evening,' he remarked when we were settled in the deep leather chairs. 'I half expected Hugo would have packed you off home before this. What does he think about friend Ray's Svengali act?'

'I didn't tell him,' I said in a low voice.

'But I thought I'd convinced you—'

'I know, but things have changed slightly. I'm not going home, even on Saturday. The St Cyrs have offered me a partnership in the Viking.'

'You mean you'll be here permanently?'

I lifted my chin. 'Yes, but don't worry; you won't be expected to go on playing knight-errant indefinitely.'

'I don't think I understand,' he said after a moment.

'Hugo told me he rather coerced you into asking me out. It was kind of you but quite unnecessary. I can take care of myself.'

His mouth tightened fractionally. 'I still

157

don't know what you're talking about, but let me clarify the position. I don't belong to an escort agency, Chloe, and my services aren't for hire. I can't see how Hugo comes into this.'

I flushed, aware that he had put me on the defensive. 'I'm sorry if I put it clumsily, but when he said—'

'I told you I had the impression he wasn't happy about your seeing Ray, but if I was supposed to take that as an all-clear to ask you out myself, I'm afraid it was completely lost on me. I asked you out for no reason other than I wanted to. If I obliged Hugo by doing so, that's fine, but it's quite coincidental. All right?'

I nodded and finished my drink in a gulp. Neil signalled to the waiter for another.

'Now that we've cleared that up, let's get back to Ray. Does he know you're staying?'

'Yes, I had my first sitting with him yesterday.' I hesitated. 'I gather he was causing a bit of trouble today?'

'He certainly was. Apparently he doesn't approve of our meeting this evening.'

My fingers tightened on the glass. 'What did he say?'

'Nothing to me; he ignored me completely, but he gave Pam one or two choice pieces of advice to pass on.'

'About me?' My voice cracked.

'I'm afraid so, yes. He can be pretty vicious, you know. I hope you know what you're doing.' He looked across at me consideringly.

'Why didn't you tell Hugo the whole story?'

'You know why; he wouldn't have let me stay.'

'In my opinion you'd be wiser not to. From the way Ray was carrying on today I'd say he was bordering on the psychopathic.'

'I'm really rather sorry for him,' I said slowly.

'*Sorry?*'

'He's so completely alone, Neil. To his way of thinking, he brought me over here expressly to have someone of his own, someone on his side, and now that I won't fall into line he's bewildered and hurt. So he lashes out.'

'He's certainly doing that. I must say you're more charitable than he deserves.'

'And then I have this horrible feeling that he's in danger, threatened in some way.'

'I shouldn't be at all surprised,' Neil returned dryly. 'After today I can think of at least six people who would cheerfully slit his throat. I could myself.'

My hand jerked sharply, spilling the liquid in my glass. With a look at my face, Neil held out a clean handkerchief and I dabbed ineffectually at the stain.

'I'm sorry, I didn't mean to upset you. That hypnotist certainly has a lot to answer for. Whatever made you go up on the stage?'

I thought back to that fateful evening. 'I think it was to annoy Mike. His father was a psychiatrist and he was being very superior about the whole thing, saying it shouldn't be allowed. Actually, we hadn't even realized a hypnotist was on the bill. Sue and I were celebrating having scraped through our O-levels and as no party had materialized, the four of us went on spec to the theatre.'

'Who was it who finally brought you round?'

I smiled. 'Ironically enough, Mike's father.'

'After three days?'

I nodded. Three days, during which my body had been inactive. But what of my mind? Where had it travelled during the trance which could overcome dimensional barriers? Here, to the Isle of Man, into its past and future, or simply deeper into the mind that held me, back to its ancient folk memories and forward by means of its possibly unrecognized clairvoyance?

Neil glanced at his watch. 'If you've finished your drink we'd better be on our way.'

As Annette had told me, the Viking by night exuded a very different atmosphere from that of my last visit. Most of the tables were occupied, I noted with professional interest, and on each one a small copper lamp glowed, leaving the rafters and the shape of the longboat in softly moving shadow. Down by the hotplates Gaston was at work carving meat and spooning out luscious-smelling casseroles.

Annette came hurrying over with the menus and greeted me with enthusiasm. 'Checking up on us? I hope we come up to expectations!'

160

When the complexities of choosing our first course had been resolved and we were alone again, I turned to Neil. 'You know, we seem to have spent a great deal of time discussing the complications of my existence but literally the only thing I know about you is that you teach at St Olaf's. I'm not even sure what subject!'

'That's easily rectified. Classics. For the rest, there's not much to tell. I enjoy my life, but it hasn't been wildly exciting.'

'What about your family?'

'Pretty standard, I imagine. My brother is a G.P., following in Father's footsteps, and my sister was married a couple of weeks ago. I'd been home for her wedding when I saw you on the plane.'

'Hugo was saying you've been at St Olaf's about six years.'

'Yes. Sometimes I wonder if that isn't long enough.'

'You're not thinking of leaving? Not when I'd just arranged to stay!'

'Not at the moment, but I'm ambitious, Chloe. Sometimes that can be the very devil. I intend to have my own school one day.'

'You sound as though Vivian has been brainwashing you!'

He laughed. 'It paid off for her, anyway. Have you heard that Nicholas landed the Downhurst post?'

'No, I hadn't. I am glad. They both seemed to regard it as their last chance.'

'I just hope the strain isn't too much for him. He's been living off his nerves for years, but this term he's worse than ever.'

Annette came back with our main courses. 'Were the recipe books all right?' she asked.

'Marvellous, thanks. I've had a busy day!'

'You're keeping your hand in, are you?' Neil commented as she moved away.

'I've been baking for the bazaar tomorrow.'

'I must say you've been incorporated into the community remarkably quickly!'

The meal was extremely good and Neil was amused by my comments as I sampled sauce and cutlet, vegetables and garnish. All of it was well up to the standards of *Les Cinq Nids* and my last doubts about accepting the partnership disappeared.

Subconsciously I relaxed and for the first time we were able to talk freely, to exchange ideas and points of view, without any hint of the supernatural overshadowing us. Neil was interested to hear about Paris and the cookery course and I laughed at stories of his brother Daniel's days at medical school. And throughout the evening the atmosphere of the Viking, with its lamplight and shadows, wrapped us round and made us welcome. I wanted it to go on for ever but one by one the tables around us emptied and I knew sadly that it could be drawn out no longer.

'It's time I took you home,' Neil said.

The wind had risen, sending wispy black

clouds scudding over the silver-grey are of the sky. Above us trees lifted skeletal arms in stark silhouette and a rustling multitude of leaves alternately advanced and retreated in the gusts that blew along the sides of the road. We reached the cottage much too soon. Neil got out and came round to open my door.

'Thank you for a lovely evening,' I said.

'I've enjoyed it too. We must do it again.' He drew me towards him and again I steeled myself to match my attitude with his. It was a gentle kiss, undemanding, uncommitted, yet surely this, I thought on a wave of longing, was what had really brought me to the island, and again I felt pity for Ray. After a moment he raised his head and looked down at me.

'Do you still imagine I asked you out to please Hugo?' he asked softly. 'If so, perhaps this will convince you otherwise.' He pulled me close again and this time the kiss was more urgent, altogether more personal. It was the memory of this, out of context, that had sent me hurrying towards him at Heathrow. For several minutes past and future hung deliriously locked in the present, until an instinct older than time alerted me to the fact that we were being watched.

I turned quickly, my eyes flying open, and gave a sharp cry. Down the lane a figure had detached itself from the shadow of the trees and was moving silently away.

Neil said urgently, 'What is it? What's the

matter?'

'Someone was there—behind that tree!'

'Watching us, you mean?' He turned sharply. 'I can't see anything. You must have imagined it.'

I didn't answer but his own denial hadn't convinced him, because he added brusquely, 'Well, I hope he enjoyed it, whoever he was.'

What had been between us was tarnished and spoilt.

'It's time you went in anyway,' he said. 'Good-night, Chloe.'

'Good-night.' I turned and walked blindly up the path to the house. 'Whoever he was' Neil had said, but I knew that neither of us doubted who it had been.

CHAPTER THIRTEEN

That night my sleep was peppered with fragments of dreams which melted away as I reached to examine them more closely: the stretch of coastline seen from the hill; a straw guy; Kirree Clegg's blue, blue eyes. I came fully awake to the memory of Ray's antagonism and Neil's spoiled kisses. It could only have been Ray, surreptitiously hidden in the shadows watching us, determined to see for himself whether I accorded Neil more than the 'arm's length treatment'. Miserably I wondered what conclusion he had reached and how it would govern his actions now.

'Evil comes home to roost': one of Granny Clegg's nebulous warnings. It seemed quite feasible that she was able to translate vibrations from Ray and myself into some identifiable threat.

The future seemed to be lying in wait for me like a giant bird of prey. On a wave of despair I wondered whether to run away again after all. Perhaps by avoiding any further unpleasantness with Ray it would be possible to avert the lurking danger which appeared to hang over us.

As for Neil, he might well decide our continuing friendship wasn't worth the trouble Ray seemed bent on causing. It was only my infernal time-jumping which had accelerated my own feelings, catapulting me to our first meeting already in love with him.

This assessment, apparently already acknowledged subconsciously, took me by surprise but I had to admit its truth. Unfortunately there was no way of knowing whether our dream relationship had progressed beyond last night. I had 'remembered' Neil's kisses; now, I had received them. That might be all that was due to me.

'I forgot to mention I have to go into college this morning,' Martha told me when, heavy-eyed, I finally reached the kitchen. 'Some folios have been mislaid and they're needed for an exhibition at the weekend. I shouldn't be long though, so we can still have an early lunch and be up at the hall by two. Is all your stuff ready?'

'Almost. I just have to assemble the *gâteau* and put the finishing touches to the cakes.'

'There's Hugo tooting. See you later.' The kitchen door banged behind her.

I drank a cup of coffee which was all the breakfast I wanted, and the hard knot of misery lay heavy and unmoving inside me. Mechanically I filled the coffee cake with whipped cream, spread fondant icing on the *japonais au chocolat* and sandwiched together the tiny meringues, decorating each with its piece of crystallized cherry. Even the delicate task of dipping the balls of choux pastry into syrup and arranging them round the Gâteau St Honoré occupied only a fraction of my attention.

After an hour or so I paused and surveyed my handiwork with a professional eye. The gingerbread and cheese scones were already stacked in tins for transporting to the hall, the *petits fours* arranged in sweetpaper casings. There was nothing more I could do for the moment.

I remember turning from the kitchen table and starting towards the hall. After that, I don't know. As I reached the door a clutch of terror inexplicably grabbed hold of me and in the same instant I seemed to see an enormous lorry, headlamps blazing, charging down the hall towards me. There was no time to question the veracity of its appearance, nor to move out of the way. I flung my arms instinctively over my head and screamed in a frenzy of fear. The next second I was thrown to the floor by the shattering impact as huge wheels crushed down on my body. Total darkness engulfed me.

I'm not sure how long I lay there before struggling back to consciousness. My arms were still clamped protectively round my head and it took a considerable effort to unlock them. Dizzily I sat up. Above me on the hall table was the vase of chrysanthemums Martha had arranged the day before. Their bitter scent pricked at my nostrils. Through the open sitting-room door I could see the fireplace and a corner of Hugo's chair. It was all so normal, so safe and familiar. How could I possibly have conjured up that mind-shattering vision of a juggernaut in this tiny hallway?

Ray! The name clarioned in my head like an alarum bell. Could I warn him in time? How many precious minutes had elapsed while I lay unconscious on the floor?

I hurled myself at the phone, all memory of our last meeting wiped from my mind. The number! What was the number? My incoherent prayers were answered in the form of a letter on college paper laying beside the phone. With trembling fingers I started to dial.

'St Olaf's College. Can I help you?'

'Could I speak to Ray Kittering, please?'

'I'm sorry, personal calls aren't allowed during school hours.'

'But it's desperately urgent! Can you at least tell me if he's there? Please!'

The secretary doubtless had previous experience of hysterical females phoning Ray, but the note of panic in my voice must have reached her. 'Just one moment, I'll see if I can contact him for you.'

There was a click in my ear. I chewed my lip in a frenzy of impatience as one second remorsely followed another. If he wasn't there, what could I do?

'Hello, staff-room?'

'Could I—is Ray there?'

The voice sharpened. 'Chloe? Is that you? It's Neil. Whatever—?'

'*Is Ray there?*' No time for normal pleasantries—no time—

'Just a minute.'

'Hello?' Ray's voice, unmistakably. Relief swamped me and I leant on the window-sill for support. 'Hello?' he repeated more loudly. 'Are you there?'

'Yes,' I whispered dryly.

'Well, what is it?'

'You're all right?'

'To the best of my knowledge. Shouldn't I be?'

I was shaking uncontrollably. 'I thought you might have had an accident.'

'Why the hell?'

'There was a lorry, one of those continental monstrosities. It came bearing down with its headlamps blazing. I was sure you'd been hurt.'

'Where was this lorry?'

Where indeed? 'I can't explain,' I said helplessly.

'Well, this concern is all very touching but it sounds somewhat garbled to me. Anyway I can't talk now, the bell's just gone. I'll phone later if you like and you can tell me about it.'

Clumsily I dropped the telephone back on its rest. Perhaps that ghastly impact lay in the future, then. Yet its threat had seemed immediate, simultaneous, and I had not been wrong before. For the first time I wondered why I had associated the danger with Ray, when it was myself the lorry had appeared to destroy. Because my hand had hurt when he cut his? Or because, on a deeper level, I'd always known he was in danger? Perhaps I'd been brought to the island in an attempt to deflect it.

Martha came hurrying home soon afterwards. 'Chloe, are you all right? I believe you rang college?'

I nodded wearily. The extreme emotional reaction to the phenomenon had drained me.

'You look pretty shaken. What happened?'

169

Stumblingly I related my experience. She frowned.

'But why should you think it was directed against Ray?'

'There's a mental link between us, Martha. I haven't told you before because you were worried enough about me already.'

'What kind of mental link?' She looked apprehensive and I couldn't blame her.

'We "tune in" to each other sometimes. The man who hypnotized me five years ago is his uncle. That's where the connection lies.'

She stared at me. 'How long have you known all this?'

I shrugged. 'It's been building up ever since I arrived. So you see it's no use you and Hugo warning me about Ray. There's not much I can do about it.'

'Or about him, apparently. I was there when the call came through and he made the most of it, I can tell you.'

I stared at her aghast, belatedly aware of far-reaching effects I'd been too distressed to recognize before. 'What happened?'

'Oh, he implied you'd made up some story just as an excuse to contact him. It was all a dig at Neil, of course. He said you'd had a row and he'd decided to finish with you, but that if you were prepared to apologize he might give you another chance.'

'Oh God,' I said tonelessly. 'And Neil?'

'He just turned and walked out of the room.

Ray would have laboured it still further but he caught my eye and shut up.'

'But you think Neil understood? I mean, he does know about this.'

'All I can tell you is that he certainly didn't look as though he understood.' She glanced across at me with compassion. 'Did he make another date with you?'

'Nothing definite.'

'Well, he'll be at the sherry party tomorrow. If I were you I should waste no time in putting the record straight. If it's important to you, that is.'

She waited to see if I'd any comment to make but I was beyond it. 'You still look groggy. Will you be able to face the bazaar?'

'It'll help to take my mind off everything. Anyway, I couldn't let Vivian down at this stage.'

'We'd better think about having some lunch, then.'

'I couldn't—'

'You'll have a bowl of soup, at least,' said my sister-in-law firmly. 'Even I can produce that, since I have a tin-opener handy! Now go and wash your face, it'll make you feel better.' She gave me a gentle little push in the direction of the bathroom and went to locate the tin of soup.

By the time we set off for St Stephen's I had at least outwardly regained my composure. Inwardly, I was struggling to hold my mind

171

above the abyss of conjecture which seethed just below the surface. I might have known Ray would lose no opportunity to humiliate either Neil or myself and I had made it ridiculously easy for him. He could never have hoped for so perfect an opening.

The road outside the church was already lined with parked cars and a little procession of women, arms piled high with boxes and tins, was wending its way round the churchyard to the hall. Martha drew up behind the last car and we too set off with our offerings.

A barrage of noise met us as we pushed open the door. Rudimentary stalls had already been erected and men up ladders were draping crepe paper and fixing the names of the different stalls. Vivian, list in hand, was directing operations.

'Chloe, what a gorgeous *gâteau*! You're an angel! Put it on the centre table, would you, with the other raffle prizes. Your stall is the third on the left, and fancy goods is at the far end, Martha.' She turned to answer a query from someone hovering near and we obediently moved away.

Martha introduced me to Sally Davidson, Linda Barton and Amy Carnforth, and in spite of myself I felt a flicker of interest at seeing Sheila Shoesmith again. She was small and fair, elfin-faced with a pointed chin and baby-blue eyes which kept blinking nervously. I wondered if she knew how widespread her most intimate secrets were.

Amy had been transferred to my stall from the overstaffed stationery section. 'Did you make all these yourself?' she asked, round-eyed. 'They look just like bought cakes!' Which comment I assumed was meant as a compliment. As Vivian had told me, several people arrived with contributions of buns and pastries and when everything was laid out the counter looked most attractive.

I was hardly aware of the actual opening of the bazaar but it gradually became apparent that people were wandering about in the body of the hall. A few children, presumably from the village school, enthusiastically partook of the Lucky Dip and the Hoop-La. They also cleared our stall of flapjacks. The vicar wandered over and Amy introduced him to me. He was obviously passionately interested in his tiny church and enquired whether I had seen the cross in the churchyard. I assured him that I had.

'Others continue the legend, you know,' he told me, 'in Andreas and Jurby, notably, and of course there's a large collection of crosses at Maughold. Fascinating, fascinating!' And he wandered happily off.

Business on the cake stall became brisker and I realized suddenly that it was five o'clock. The boys from St Olaf's had arrived and in their wake the masters and those wives not actively engaged in running the bazaar. I tried to keep an eye open for Neil, but the hall was now crowded and it was impossible to see who was there. In any event he didn't come near our stall. With the last scone sold and the money duly counted, Amy and I were free to move round to see what was left. Not much was; the bare tables were proof of a profitable afternoon. My legs were aching from standing for so long and probably as a result of my trauma that morning, my head had started to throb with dull persistency.

'Chloe!' Martha was at my side. 'Your cakes were a wow! Everyone's talking about them.

'How soon can we get away?'

'The raffle will be drawn at six—in about ten minutes—and after that we can go. We just hand the money and price tickets to Vivian and hope they tally! The men dismantle the stalls so we don't have to see to that.'

'Is Hugo here?'

'No, he suggested it would be more sensible if he went straight home and had dinner waiting for us.'

The raffle was duly drawn and the prizes distributed. None of my tickets was of any use. With the empty cake tins under my arm I followed Martha thankfully into the cold darkness. It had started to rain. I should be glad when today was over.

Hugo had banked up the fire and the sitting-room was cosy and welcoming. He came to the kitchen door to greet us, one of

Martha's aprons round his waist.

'How did it go? You look tired, both of you. Go and sit down and I'll pour you a drink.'

Gratefully I eased myself into one of the large comfortable chairs and kicked off my shoes.

'Chops for dinner,' Hugo said rallyingly, putting a glass into my hand. 'I vote we have it on trays round the fire this evening.' He glanced at me. 'All right, Chloe? There were one or two odd comments buzzing about today which I couldn't quite follow.'

'She phoned Ray during break this morning,' Martha said quietly.

Hugo raised an eyebrow. 'Hardly wise, surely? And I thought you'd had a row?'

Resignedly, because I could no longer postpone it, I embarked at last on the full story of my involvement with Ray, incorporating entirely without embellishment my forays into other time-bands. Hugo and Martha listened in growing incredulity, while behind the drawn curtains the rain lashed against the windows and occasionally fell down the chimney to land hissing on the burning logs.

When at last I stopped speaking silence flooded over us in a suffocating wave. Finally Hugo cleared his throat.

'I don't know what to say. I thought there was more to it all than you'd told us, but this! It's mind-bending! I'd say there's no doubt, though, that it all stems from the hypnotism. I remember reading that some parapsychologists use it to develop extra-sensory perception. But how on earth you've kept it all to yourself—'

'I told Neil,' I said quietly.

'What was his reaction?'

'That I should go home straight away.'

'Good advice. I don't like this at all, Chloe. There's no saying where it will end.'

'It won't go on much longer, I know that.'

He looked at me sharply. 'What do you mean?'

'I'm not sure, except—' That Ray's days were numbered. I couldn't say it, couldn't put into words the threat of that black cloud in case by so doing I made its approach inevitable. I shook my head helplessly.

'Lord, what an appalling mess! What the hell are we going to do? I suppose we could always try to find that man again, get him to release you.'

'That's what Neil said; that if I actively tried to free myself it might work this time. On the other hand, though—' I broke off.

'What?'

'It could go the other way. I could sink so far into his mind that I disappeared without trace, mentally speaking. For good.'

Into the charged silence which greeted my words the telephone jangled discordantly. With a glance at Hugo, Martha went to answer it. She turned to me, her hand over the mouthpiece.

'Talk of the devil—it's Ray. He sounds a bit odd.'

I took the receiver from her. 'Hello?'

'Chloe?' His voice was wrongly pitched.

'Yes?'

'We've just received a phone call from the mainland. Uncle Tom was killed this morning. A Belgian pantechnicon knocked him down just after ten o'clock.'

CHAPTER FOURTEEN

Tom Kelly was dead. It had been his anguish and not Ray's that had subconsciously flashed me that urgent S.O.S. and now his help was beyond my reach. His death may, of course, have fused the currents running between Ray and myself, but it seemed more likely that it would simply remove the obstruction he'd imposed, leaving me still more vulnerable to Ray's influence.

The meeting with the St Cyrs was arranged for Hugo's free period that morning and there could hardly have been a less appropriate time to discuss my future. Hugo and Martha had been as shaken as I by the dramatic fulfilment of my premonition.

'I really think we should postpone this meeting,' Hugo began worriedly. 'Instead of committing yourself to an indefinite stay it would be more sensible to go home while you still can.'

I shook my head. 'Running away won't solve anything. It never has, though it's taken me a long time to realize it.'

'But I keep thinking of the dreams you told us about. Suppose they really were precognitive?'

'I wonder,' I said musingly, 'how much the future can be changed by foreknowledge.'

'Not being a quantum physicist, I have no idea.'

'I know I can't escape it altogether but I might be able to divert the danger like I did for John.' It was little comfort, but it was all I had.

So we kept our appointment at the Viking, the details of the partnership were agreed and it was decided I should start work in a week's time. Hugo dropped me at the cottage on his way back to college and Martha was waiting for me at the door.

'Ray's here,' she said briefly. 'He insists on seeing you.'

He was standing at the sitting-room window and turned as I entered. I was shocked at the drawn look on his face. Perhaps, despite their estrangement, he had still cared for Tom Kelly.

'I'm sorry about your uncle.' I looked across at him warily, trying to test the atmosphere between us, but he brushed my condolences aside.

'You thought that lorry was meant for me, didn't you? Why? It could as easily have been yourself, surely?'

'Yes, except that the shock waves it created were there, in the atmosphere, so I assumed it had already happened.'

'And when I came to the phone?'

'It seemed I'd been wrong. I never even thought of Tom Kelly.'

He lit a cigarette, not meeting my eyes. 'In your place I doubt if I'd have bothered with the warning, after the way I behaved the other day.'

'And you didn't believe me, anyway. Martha said you proclaimed to all and sundry it was just an excuse to contact you.'

'Yes, well I'm sorry about that, but it was such a smack in the eye for Neil Sheppard. Didn't I tell you it was not for his benefit I brought you here?'

With an effort I unflexed my fingers. 'And why are you here now?'

He smiled sourly. 'To offer the olive branch, why else? There's nothing to be gained by fighting each other and I want you with me this evening. I'm tired of the role of lone wolf.'

But this evening I had to make my peace with Neil.

'And tomorrow,' he added deliberately, 'we have another sitting, remember.'

'Which,' I said heavily, 'is the real reason

179

you came. You knew you'd gone too far and you were afraid I'd refuse to sit for you.'

'Ah, come on now, would I be as devious as that?' But he was smiling.

'You would, and I can't imagine why I let you get away with it. Except, perhaps, that I had no choice?'

'Don't be hard on me, Chloe. You're the only friend I have.'

'You've only yourself to blame for that. Why do you have to keep antagonizing people? It's so unnecessary.' *And so dangerous.* Even though the lorry had not, after all, been meant for him, there was still a threat somewhere, something more deliberate and personal than a random traffic accident. I added urgently, 'Ray, please make an effort to be nicer to people. I'm sure they'd meet you halfway.'

'Still bent on reforming me, are you? Sure, it's too late for that.'

'You could try. Remember what Granny Clegg said, about evil coming home to roost.'

'Ah, she's just a superstitious old woman. Why should I worry my head about her? But if you're going to start preaching I'm off. I've skipped one class as it is, but I needed to see you. Till this evening, then.'

Only when he had gone did I realize the full extent of my foolishness in agreeing to be with him that evening but at the same time I was aware of a sense of the inevitable. Try as I might I could not desert Ray, and any chance to speak privately to Neil must be seized as and when it offered itself. I was not looking forward to the sherry party.

Having parked the car in the usual place, Hugo led Martha and myself across the brilliantly floodlit quadrangle to the Stanley Room where the gathering was being held. Just inside the door the headmaster and his wife awaited their guests. Harold Leadbetter B.Sc., Eton and Cambridge, was a rotund and jovial-looking man.

'Delighted, delighted!' he murmured over my hand as Hugo introduced me. His wife smiled vaguely at his side and at a discreet distance Frank Harrison and his wife carried out their duties of deputy headship. This was the man who, according to Vivian, had usurped Nicholas's rightful place. Tall and bland-faced, with carefully smoothed hair and horn-rimmed spectacles, he appeared far better suited to the position than poor Nicholas. In all probability the headmaster was not as foolish as Vivian imagined.

One of the prefects approached with a tray of sherry glasses. 'Sweet or dry, Miss Winter?' I looked at him in surprise and he added shyly, 'You will come and sit for us again, won't you?' It was one of my youthful portrait painters. My presence on the island was certainly being well documented, I thought with a touch of grim humour.

'Chloe, may I introduce you to Mrs

181

Hibbard?' Carol Fenton was claiming my attention and as I smiled and exchanged pleasantries I caught sight of Neil across the room and my mouth went dry. With a murmured excuse I started to make my way towards him, but almost immediately Sally Davidson caught my arm and drew me into her group.

'Will you show me sometime how to make some of those gorgeous things you produced yesterday? Philip's been glassy-eyed with admiration ever since!'

Her husband laughed. 'Never mind the fancy things, just wean her away from macaroni cheese and you'll be my friend for life! Do you know everyone, by the way? I don't think you've met David?'

He was good-looking; tall and broad-shouldered, with thick black hair and regular features. More brawn than brain, Ray had said, and like a materialization of the memory he came up and took my arm.

'Meeting David, my sweet? As I told you, he's an expert in all branches of sport, indoors and out. The rest of us are continually amazed by his—stamina!'

At my side Sheila Shoesmith started nervously and David's handsome, rather solid face suffused with dark colour. I held my breath as his fist clenched into a ball but he regained control of himself and, turning on his heel, shouldered his way through the crowd leaving everyone avoiding each other's eyes.

'Was it something I said?' Ray asked in mock dismay.

Philip said tightly, 'Be thankful he didn't close your mouth for you. It's time someone did. I warn you, Ray, we've had just about as much as we can take.'

'Well, that was quite a speech! I hope such loyalty's appreciated. It seems an underrated commodity these days.' His bantering gaze moved idly in Sheila's direction, but as Philip took a menacing step forward he put up his hand with a laugh. 'All right, just going! Dear me, how touchy everyone is this evening!'

With his arm firmly through mine he drew me perforce away with him. I looked over my shoulder with a helpless glance of apology, but the faces that met me were no longer friendly.

I said in a rush, 'If that's how you're going to behave, I'm washing my hands of you here and now.'

'You may want to, my love, but you can't. We're stuck with each other, you and I, for better, for worse as the Good Book says—and it'll probably be worse! Now, look who we have here!'

We had come face to face with Neil and Pam Beecham. Ray's arm tightened fractionally on mine. Pam's eyes were sullen and hostile and as I turned to Neil I saw at once how much ground had been lost. His face was politely formal.

'Good evening, Chloe. I hear your efforts at the bazaar were greatly appreciated.' And with a vague, dismissive smile he piloted Pam away.

I stood fighting back helpless tears and at my side Ray said softly, 'Well, well! Quite a change from the passionate embrace, wasn't it?'

I spun to face him and something in my expression jolted him into sudden awareness. 'And it really matters, doesn't it?' he added flatly. 'Blast his eyes!'

I said rapidly, 'Can you attach yourself to someone else for a while?' and, seeing a door across the room, quickly made my way towards it before he could reply.

A dimly lit corridor stretched away in the direction of some classrooms. On my left a small door was marked 'Cloakroom' and beneath it a temporary notice, presumably just for this evening, added 'Ladies'. I hesitated, wondering if a splash of cold water would cool my burning cheeks, and as I stood there a door lower down opened and Neil came out, stopping abruptly as he caught sight of me.

'I didn't follow you,' I said dully.

'My dear Chloe, it never occurred to me that—'

'But since you're here, could you spare me a moment?'

'Certainly. Shall we go back inside?'

'No.' Firmly I stood my ground. 'It's easier to talk here, without interruptions.'

'Very well.'

'Neil, I'm sorry about that phone call.'

He raised an eyebrow. 'Yesterday, you mean? Why?'

'I didn't mean to brush you aside like that, but I was in such a panic—'

He moved impatiently. 'I think I'm the one who should apologize. I was so intent on "saving" you from Ray that it never struck me you might not want saving.'

I shook my head. 'Please try to understand. It was that horrible telepathy again.' I paused but he made no attempt to help me. 'I had a kind of vision of a huge lorry rushing straight at me and I couldn't get out of the way.' It sounded unconvincing, even to myself. 'I passed out,' I added expressionlessly. He frowned but made no comment. 'When I came round I was sure it was happening to Ray.'

I searched his face for a sign that there was still something left between us, but he was feeling in his pocket for cigarettes.

'Well, since he's quite safe you can relax, can't you? There was no need to explain; it's none of my business, after all.'

'I'm sorry,' I said tightly, 'I thought it was.' I braced myself to meet his eyes. 'For the record,' I added in a rush, 'it was Ray's uncle who was run over yesterday morning.' And I turned blindly into the dubious haven of the ladies' cloakroom. I think that as I closed the door I heard him say, 'Chloe!' but I can't be

185

sure. I stood with my hands gripping the sides of the basin willing myself not to break down completely. Quite obviously I was more trouble than I was worth and Ray was welcome to me. My attempt at an apology had only made things worse.

After a minute or two I straightened and studied my reflection in the mirror. Apart from heightened colour, attributable anyway to the heat in the crowded room, I looked remarkably normal. Which was as well, for at that moment the door was pushed open and two girls came in, chattering gaily. I gave them a bright, unseeing smile and made my way back to the party.

Fortunately I found Martha almost at once. 'Sherry, for the love of Allah!' I said in an undertone. Surprised, she handed me her own glass and I drained it at a gulp and helped us both to another from a passing tray.

'It's Neil, isn't it?' she said shrewdly. 'What happened?'

'Nothing,' I answered, 'Nothing at all.'

She took my arm and led me firmly to the nearest group. 'I don't think you know Claudine Bouchet ...'

The evening ground on. A buffet was served but my throat was closed and it was useless to try to eat. Ray reappeared. Faces swam in and out of focus, voices jabbered meaninglessly, but I kept my smile fixed and no-one suspected my disorientation. At last the ordeal was over. We said our good-byes—to Vivian and Nicholas, to the Fentons, to the headmaster and his deputy, and as I climbed with infinite weariness into the back of Hugo's car I remembered the hopes with which I had left it. I had been so sure everything would be all right once I'd explained to Neil, and I had been so abysmally wrong.

That night I experienced another of my time-switches and this time there was one important difference: I was recognized.

It was Laa'll Katrina, St Catherine's Eve, at Colby Fair. This much I somehow knew, but even in this uncertain past my present-day troubles had followed me and I was miserable, confused and afraid. I stood on the outskirts of the crowd watching with no flicker of curiosity as a procession of boys marched round the fairground carrying what appeared to be a dead hen. After a while they sat down on the ground and embarked on a ritual plucking ceremony and everyone surged forward, seemingly intent on securing one of the black feathers. There was much good-humoured jostling and after a moment one or two young men broke away and ran off in the direction of the inn, waving feathers as though these were tokens enabling them to free drinks.

The girls, however, seemed to put a more romantic significance on acquiring a feather and my eyes were full of tears of self-pity as I watched them laughing and dodging about.

Suddenly one of them spun round with a cry of triumph, holding aloft a handful of feathers, and, pursued by her companions, came running towards me. By this time I no longer expected anyone to notice me during my invasions of the past, and although the girl was running straight towards me I made no attempt to move. To my surprise, however, she skidded to a halt, gazing directly at me with widening eyes.

Her pursuing friends caught up and surrounded her. 'What is it then, Bridie? What are you looking at? Give us some of your feathers, now! Isn't one husband enough for you?'

But Bridie remained transfixed staring at me and I stared back, aware of a niggling pinprick of familiarity about the bright black eyes, Then with a jolt memory sickeningly asserted itself, etching wrinkles in the smooth olive skin, drying and fading the vibrant black hair, and I realized with a sense of disbelief that I was looking at the Granny Clegg of sixty years ago—and that she recognized me! For the first time in my visits to the half-world of the past I had been seen and known for myself.

'Bridie!' The girls were becoming impatient. 'Are you after seeing a ghost, then? Ah, leave her be, Joaney, her wits are addled!' and they turned after more interesting game. I waited, motionless, and slowly, moving as though strings jerked at her limbs, she came

188

towards me until only a few feet separated us. Then, with a singularly sweet smile in which I could read both sympathy and encouragement, she held out to me one of her precious black feathers.

Seconds later on my return to Hugo's guest-room I searched for it diligently and was almost surprised not to find it.

CHAPTER FIFTEEN

The loss of that feather from another dimension assumed a morbid significance from which I could not free myself. Had I been able to hold on to it, all would have come right between Neil and myself. As it was, there was probably no hope.

In the meantime I had committed myself to the sitting with Ray, and though I hoped that wet weather might release me from it, the day dawned uncaringly brilliant, blue and gold with frost on the grass and wraiths of mist disappearing over the hills. There was to be no reprieve; I should have to suppress my uneasiness and sit again for Ray.

'I'm sorry about last night,' he said as he started up the car.

'What in particular?' I didn't want to think about last night.

'I gather that bastard Sheppard slapped you

189

down. He's got one hell of a temper, hasn't he? We nearly came to blows later.'

I drew a deep breath. 'Ray, what exactly are you trying to say?'

'I didn't realize you'd had a word with him yourself, but I saw he'd upset you so I tackled him about it.'

I wasn't surprised Neil had lost his temper. He was hardly likely to submit to being taken to task by Ray. He must be wishing most heartily that he had never set eyes on me.

'Promise me something?' I said after a moment.

'What?'

'Not to mention Neil Sheppard for the rest of the day.'

'With the greatest of pleasure.'

We drove to the spot where we had parked before and climbed the hill with our accoutrements. Ray was quieter than usual and I was incapable of small talk. Within minutes I had settled myself on the canvas stool, the stole draped round my shoulders and my face turned resolutely to the sea. I hoped he would not be working on my eyes; they were not at their best that day.

The coast of Ireland was obscured by a gauzy haze, but nearer at hand several small boats bobbed on the blue water and, as ever, the gulls circled and wheeled, circled and wheeled, their haunting cries floating back to earth like the lament of lost souls.

'You're very subdued today,' I remarked during our coffee break. 'What's the matter?'

He glanced up, then away and out to sea. 'I've been indulging in a bout of self-analysis and it's not all that edifying.'

'It doesn't sound like one of your pastimes.'

'You forced me into it, with some of the home truths you were handing out yesterday.'

'And what conclusions did you reach?'

He smiled briefly. 'Chiefly, that if I'm to get anywhere at all with you I'll have to take myself in hand.'

'Ray—'

'Yes, I know: Neil Sheppard's the light of your life at the moment but I don't hold out much hope in that direction. He's as stubborn as a mule and if I didn't get through to him last night, nothing will. So all being equal you may yet settle for me if I change my spots in time. And if you did, I wouldn't need to be so bitter and twisted anyway.' He stood up and tipped the dregs of his coffee on to the grass. 'But enough of this philosophizing! Back to work!'

We took up our positions again and another couple of hours passed. By way of a mental censorship I was concentrating on planning a series of exotic dishes for my first week at the Viking.

'I'll have to start looking for somewhere to live,' I said aloud.

'Digs, you mean?'

'I'd rather buy a cottage if I can find

something suitable.'

'It'll be pricey. Property's expensive over here.'

'So I believe.' I shifted my position slightly. 'My back's stiff. Isn't it time for lunch?'

'We can stop now if you like.'

We ate in an almost companionable silence. Despite my misgivings and against all odds, we seemed to be back on a more or less firm footing.

'You can take a few more minutes if you like,' he remarked as I prepared to return to my stool. 'I'm not satisfied with the coastline so I'll be working on that for a while. Go and stretch your legs while you have the chance. I'll call when I need you.'

Glad of the extended respite I walked over the uneven ground and stood for a minute or two watching the boats far out to sea. At my feet a sheep-track ambled away down the seaward side of the hill and I started to follow it aimlessly, the wind lessening as I dropped below the level of the hill. Eventually the track petered out on a small grass-covered ledge.

I sat down cautiously, resting my back against the warm rock. The hill behind protected me from the strong off-shore wind and there was still warmth in the late October sun. The incandescence of sun and water hurt my tender eyes and I closed them. I had not slept well the night before and almost without realizing it, drifted into a deliciously soothing doze punctuated by the mewling gulls until one cry, louder than the rest, brought me fully awake. Ahead of me the sun still danced on the water. I leaned my head back, looking up the slope of the hill behind me—and my heart seemed to freeze. While I'd slept the wind had dropped and a curtain of mist had descended, draping itself over the top of the hill while the lower slopes remained bathed in sunshine. Mist on the hill!

I scrambled to my feet, my heart suddenly clattering at the base of my throat. Why hadn't Ray called me? He surely couldn't be painting in this! And in that moment I knew that he had called, that the cry which had jolted me awake had come neither from the gulls nor over the shrouded hilltop but from inside my own head.

A cold sickness gripped me as I started back at a stumbling run up the sheeptrack, frightened out of all proportion by the sudden descent of the mist. Within a few feet the sunlight disappeared and the drifting barrier came down to enfold me, clogging eyes and mouth with its smothering grey moisture.

'Ray? Where are you?' My voice met only walls of whiteness which blocked it, closing it in. Surely if I continued along this track I should come to the painting site; but I remembered vaguely that on the way down the track had forked and I couldn't in my panic recall which direction I had taken. The ground was beginning to level under my feet. He couldn't be far away.

'Please answer, Ray!' I plunged forward and at once stumbled and nearly fell. At my feet was the stool I had been sitting on that morning, my handbag still propped against its foot. I retrieved the bag and with hands outstretched like a sleepwalker moved on until my recoiling fingers touched the framework of the easel. Edging my way round it, the breath tearing at my lungs, I was confronted by my own face, hair blowing, eyes dreaming. A loaded paintbrush rested on the palette at my feet and half hidden beneath it, dulled by a bloom of moisture, lay a small cigarette lighter. I picked it up and slipped it into the deep pocket of my skirt.

He couldn't have gone without me, surely? Perhaps he had set out to look for me and become lost as I had in the mist. My skirt brushed against his stool and I sank weakly on to it, but there was latent disadvantage in being below normal height in this floating blindness and I stood up quickly. I drew breath to call again but the mist thrust cotton-wool fingers down my throat stifling the unborn cry and in the same moment I realized I was no longer alone. Someone, as in my dream, was waiting there in the mist. For me?

Instinctively I started to edge away but the clumsy movement wound the folds of my long skirt about my legs and I tugged at it to free myself. Where was Ray? What had happened? And what was there about this moment in time that it should have transported itself to me in advance by way of warning? Was I about to die?

Inches away a twig snapped and with it the last of my self-control. With only the vaguest sense of direction I flung myself forward, sobbing and choking with terror, wrenching my ankle on the uneven stony path, slipping and sliding in a frenzy of escape. Down, down to the blessed sunshine—nothing else mattered. Once out in the clear air the danger would miraculously melt away. If I could see, I should no longer be afraid. And it was then, with safety almost reached, that I saw him through the thinning strands of mist, the man from my dream turning slowly to face me, blocking off my descent.

The scream tore itself from my throat before I was aware of its conception and high above me in the invisible sky the gulls echoed it mockingly. It was still ringing in my head as I felt my arms seized and shaken and a voice, hoarse with shock, demanded urgently, 'Chloe! Chloe for God's sake what's the matter?'

It was Neil.

My knees gave way and as I sagged he caught me up, holding me against his body for support. 'What happened?' he repeated. 'Are you hurt?'

Wordlessly I shook my head, the abrupt

cessation of fear too swift for me.

'Is Ray with you?'

'I can't find him,' I said, and burst into tears.

'Then I'd better take you home. What frightened you so much?'

'Someone was up there.'

'Apart from Ray, you mean? Stop crying now and tell me what happened.'

Incoherently I explained about leaving Ray painting and the mist coming down while I slept.

'And he wasn't there when you got back?'

'No, that's what I can't understand. But someone was.'

'You saw him?'

'No. He stepped on a twig and I panicked and ran.'

'Your imagination was probably playing tricks by that time,' Neil said gently, 'and I'm not surprised. I must say it was very irresponsible of Ray to go off like that. I hope for his sake he has a plausible explanation.'

My breath was steadying now, the tears drying on my cheeks, and it was beginning to dawn on me that this solicitous questioning was a distinct improvement on the cool rebuff of last night.

A very few steps brought us to the final outposts of the mist and incredibly, as I'd almost stopped believing, the sun still shone. Neil's car was parked at the foot of the hill, next to Ray's. I came to a halt.

'You see! He can't have gone!'

'I spotted his car from the main road. That's why I stopped.'

'But if he hasn't gone and he isn't up there, where is he?' My voice was beginning to rise again. Briskly Neil opened his car door and gave me a little push. 'In!'

'But I can't just go off and leave him!'

'It seems he went off and left you. We could leave a note if you've any paper with you.'

I opened my bag, which surprisingly I hadn't dropped in my headlong flight, and tore a page from the diary. On it I scribbled, 'Lost you in the mist so am going home. Chloe.' I handed it to Neil, who wedged it behind the windscreen wipers of the blue Renault. A moment later he was beside me and we were bumping over the rough ground to the main road.

'What were you doing here anyway?' I asked curiously.

After a moment's silence he said levelly, 'I had you on my conscience. I didn't behave too well last night, did I?'

I bit my lip. 'I'm afraid I made rather a fool of myself.'

'No, it was I who did that and as you guessed it was because of that phone call. It was the timing of it that was so fatal. I'd been thinking about you continuously since I'd left you the previous evening, and all at once it seemed that I may have been getting things out of proportion.' I felt him glance sideways at me but I was incapable of saying anything. 'So I decided to keep my distance for a while. Then last night, when you explained what had happened, you disappeared before I'd had a chance to take it all in. Ironically enough, it was Ray who got through to me. I saw red at the time, but he was quite right.'

'He told me you almost came to blows.'

He smiled fleetingly. 'If it's any consolation I had a pretty bad night and I called round at lunch time to apologize. Martha told me you were having a sitting and roughly where, so I drove in this direction on the off-chance that you might have finished, and happened to catch sight of Ray's car. Then I noticed that the hilltop was covered in mist and remembered the dream you'd told me about, so I came up to look for you. About Ray, though; is that sinister bond between you finished now that his uncle's dead?'

'I don't think so. I heard him calling just now. That's what woke me.'

'Heard him?'

'In my head, I mean.' I shuddered. 'Up there in the mist it was exactly as I'd dreamt it, even to you appearing suddenly in front of me.' I paused. 'In the dream, you were part of the danger.'

But Neil was not to be distracted by discussing my dreams. 'You know, I think Ray's really fond of you, in which case letting fly at me on your behalf was decidedly out of

198

character.' Again the quick, interrogative glance. 'I know I keep coming back to this, but you are quite sure your feelings for him haven't changed?'

'I'm sorry for him,' I said quietly, 'but that's all.'

'You're sure about that?'

'Quite, quite sure.'

He drew a deep breath. 'And you'll forgive me for being such an idiot last night?'

I could only nod in reply but it seemed to satisfy him.

Hugo was in the garden when we stopped at the gate. His first glance must have taken in my tear-stained face, because he came quickly and opened the car door.

'You found her, then.'

'Yes. Ray'd gone off somewhere and the mist came down, so I thought I'd better bring her back.'

'Thanks very much. All right, honey?'

'More or less. I'll feel better when I know where Ray got to.'

'He'll probably phone when he gets back. Come in, Neil. You're welcome to stay for supper if you'll take pot luck.'

Looking back on that evening it stands out like a small oasis of happiness between my previous misery and the grief and suspicions that were to follow. The warmth of the room and my happiness in being with Neil combined to create in me an almost drugged state of euphoria, so that although I was expecting a phone call from Ray, I was not unduly worried when it didn't come.

When it was time for Neil to go and I went with him to the front door he held me for a moment and kissed me gently. 'I won't press my luck any further at the moment, but I'll be back. All forgiven now?'

'All forgiven,' I replied, and there was a deep well of thankfulness inside me as I closed the door behind him.

CHAPTER SIXTEEN

Since there was no morning chapel at college that Sunday, Martha and Hugo and I again attended St Stephen's. By now I recognized several people in the congregation and the vicar had a word with me after the service. My roots on the island were already beginning to go down.

It was as I was straining the vegetables for lunch that the telephone rang and a few minutes later Hugo came into the kitchen. 'That was Len Bennett from Staff House,' he told me. 'Apparently Ray hasn't turned up yet.'

I dropped the wooden spoon and turned to face him. 'You mean he's been missing all night?'

'It seems so. He wasn't in for an evening

meal but no-one thought anything of that. Saturday evenings are a bit haphazard anyway. Neil was the only one who'd have placed any importance on his absence, and of course he was here. When Ray didn't appear at breakfast someone went to his room and found the bed hadn't been slept in. No-one seems to have seen him since he left to come here yesterday morning. So Neil drove Len to the painting site—they're just back now. The car's still there and all the painting equipment, but no sign of Ray.'

'We must go back at once.' I started fumbling with the strings of my apron. 'Perhaps he went looking for me and slipped over the cliff. He could have concussion or a broken leg or something.' Further than that I dared not think.

'There's no point in rushing there straight away. Neil and Len had a pretty thorough search round all the most likely places.'

'But Hugo, I must go! If I hadn't left him when I did—'

'We'll have lunch first,' my brother said firmly. 'Then if you insist I'll drive you over so you can satisfy yourself that he isn't lying injured somewhere.'

'I always knew something would happen to him. How could I have fallen asleep like that? If only I'd stayed with him nothing would have happened.'

'You might have disappeared, too,' Hugo

retorted grimly.

'What do you mean?'

'Only that I'm increasingly thankful that Neil arrived when he did and brought you home. Now, are you going to serve lunch or must I do it myself?'

In view of Hugo's insistence I served the meal and even managed a few mouthfuls of the lamb I'd put in the oven so light-heartedly before we went to church. Neither Hugo nor Martha ate any more than I did. At one stage I said aloud, 'He can't just have disappeared!' No-one contradicted me.

By unspoken assent we piled the dishes in the sink and left them. It was a grey day, without either yesterday's sunshine or its treacherous mists. Ray's car already had a deserted air about it. My note, sodden with the overnight rain, was still on the windscreen. Followed by Hugo and Martha I set off up the hill at a run.

The picture was ruined. The colours had run together so that blue tears seemed to course down my painted cheeks in uncanny prophecy. What sudden emergency could have forced Ray to abandon his precious painting—and me?

Still shadowed by Hugo and Martha I made a quick detour of the hill-top, peering fearfully over the steeper faces to the ground far beneath. Then disconsolately I turned back to the sad wreck of the painting, feeling that it was up to me to salvage what I could of Ray's scattered belongings. But before I could touch anything a voice behind me said sharply, 'Just leave everything as it is, if you don't mind, miss.'

I turned to see the blue uniform of Ramsey police force coming up over the brow of the hill.

'My sister was here yesterday, with Mr Kittering,' Hugo explained to the man in charge.

'Ah, so you're the young lady, Miss. Perhaps I could have your name and address.'

Hugo gave me a small nod of encouragement and the policeman wrote it down. 'Now, can you tell me in your own words the circumstances leading up to the disappearance?'

'Nothing led up to it!' I said a little wildly. 'I just left Ray painting the background and went for a walk. He said he'd call when he was ready for me. I sat on a ledge for a while and—fell asleep in the sunshine. When I woke the mist was covering the top of the hill and—and Ray'd gone.'

'And roughly how long was it from the time you left Mr Kittering until you came back here?'

'I don't know. Twenty minutes, perhaps.'

'You arrived here in Mr Kittering's car?'

'Yes.'

'And how did you get home?'

'Neil Sheppard came. He took me back.'
Neil's name and address were noted in turn.

'At what stage did this Mr Sheppard arrive?'

'I met him when I was running back down the hill.'

'Running? In the mist?'

I moistened my lips. 'I was frightened. I thought someone was up here but I couldn't see anything.'

'The mist can play strange tricks at times. We'll be taking a statement from Mr Sheppard, of course. Perhaps he—'

'How will that help? He wasn't even up here.' I became aware that as we were talking a group of men had spread out over the hilltop and begun a systematic search, beating at the gorse bushes and clumps of bracken. The idea that Ray might be beneath one of them brought nausea to my throat. Hugo took my arm.

'My sister is naturally very upset by all this, Sergeant. Would it be all right if I took her home?'

'Of course, sir. We'll send a woman police officer round this evening to take her statement more formally. When we've finished here we'll be cordoning off the area.'

'Can't I take the portrait with me?' I asked wistfully.

'I'm afraid not, Miss. It will have to be tested for fingerprints, though I doubt if there's much hope of finding any after all the rain last night.'

'Finger-prints? But why—?'

'We've been asked to search for a missing person,' the police sergeant replied stolidly. 'You yourself thought someone was up here. If we can find out who that was, it might make a few things clearer.'

'Yes. Yes, I see.'

'Come along, Chloe,' Hugo said gently. 'There's nothing we can do here.'

Neil was waiting at the gate when we reached the cottage. He caught and held me as I stumbled from the car. 'You've been to the hill?'

'Chloe insisted. The police arrived while we were there.'

'Yes, I heard Len phoning them. It's incredible, isn't it? I can't seem to take it in.'

'People do disappear, though. You read of loving husbands slipping out to the corner shop for a packet of fags and never being seen again.'

'But not here!' Neil insisted. 'It's not easy to disappear on an island.'

We went into the house together and the four of us washed the lunch dishes, falling over each other in the small kitchen but thankful to have something to occupy us. We didn't talk much. I was remembering my first sight of Ray from the kitchen window and the impression I'd received of a shadow hovering over him. Sickly I knew that shadow had caught up with him.

The afternoon wore on. At about five there was a phone call for Neil to say the police were waiting at Staff House to interview him and he left immediately. Soon after a police woman, fair and neat in her uniform, arrived to take down my statement. She read back what she'd written and I signed it. It all seemed frighteningly formal, the kind of procedure familiar from police serials on television, but which you never expect to experience personally.

By nine o'clock I was exhausted. At Martha's suggestion I took some asprin and went to bed.

When Martha casually mentioned the next morning that the sitting-room was due for a thorough cleaning, I set to work dusting, polishing and sweeping in a frenzy of frustrated energy, but the remorseless circling of my fears would not be blotted out.

'I'll come with you to the life class if you like,' I offered at lunch time. 'I don't want to stay here alone and you said the boys need another sitting.'

'Fine. Thanks.' After a moment she added, 'I wonder who'll take over Ray's classes. I'll probably have to go in full-time for a while.'

'Until he turns up,' I said carefully.

'Of course. That's what I meant.'

There was an air of unhealthy excitement about the college that afternoon, a whispering in corridors and excited speculation in the classroom which broke off abruptly when we went in. It was obvious that everyone from the youngest boy upwards was well aware that I had been with Ray on Saturday. Everywhere I went I was conscious of eyes following me, speculating, wondering. I began to regret my impulse to accompany Martha.

The lesson finished at last and I went with her to the staff-room. Here the atmosphere was supercharged with tension, no-one quite meeting anyone else's eye. Only Neil's steadying smile comforted me. Nicholas Quayle came over with odd, disjointed little murmurs of concern for my alarming experience; Phyllis Lathom gave my hand a brief consoling pat when I went for my tea.

I looked round their uneasy faces: Philip, who had heatedly warned Ray to stop his scandalmongering; David Clay, who had left the group under his taunting; Pam, whom he'd reduced to tears; John Stevens, Mark Cunningham—even Hugo and Neil. Not one among them had liked Ray. Perhaps, though they could never admit it, they were relieved that he had gone.

The pervading sense of unease followed us home and supper was a silent meal. Hugo seemed wrapped in his own thoughts and when Martha twice had to repeat a question, she put a hand on his arm. 'Has anything happened, darling? Something you haven't told us?'

He stirred unhappily. 'Nothing very definite, but I'm afraid things seem to be taking a rather more serious turn. Apparently the forensic boys were up there today. There's a rumour going round that minute traces of blood were found.'

Detachedly I watched the colour leave Martha's face.

'Oh God.' She swallowed, glancing at me. 'It's a wonder they found it after all that rain.'

'It was on the canvas stool, apparently. You know how these people work, scraping up things no-one else can even see and being able to tell someone's life history from them.'

Martha's tongue moved over her lips. 'Do you gather they're treating it as a case of murder now?'

The words rattled uselessly against my eardrums. I heard them; I even understood them, but I couldn't assimilate them. On the other hand, they were what I'd subconsciously been waiting to hear since Saturday afternoon.

Hugo met my entirely empty gaze. 'It wouldn't surprise me. After all, they're pretty certain he didn't simply have an accident, or he'd have been found long before this. If he'd left voluntarily everyone seems to agree he'd have taken the painting, and certainly his car. And if he'd had a sudden brainstorm and rushed down the hill into the sea, his body would have been washed up by now. His family

208

hasn't heard from him and there's been no sign of him at the docks or airport. He's— simply vanished into thin air.'

Martha's eyes swivelled to me and I knew what she was thinking. If it was indeed murder, I was presumably the last person to have seen Ray alive.

The doorbell rang and we all started guiltily. Hugo and I were still at the table when Martha came back with Detective-Inspector Quiggin.

This time the questioning was in far greater detail. What had Ray and I been talking about during the sitting and over lunch? What kind of mood had he been in?

'I gather there's been some unpleasantness between Mr Kittering and several other members of St Olaf's staff. Did he refer specifically to any of them?'

From a long way off I heard myself say, 'I don't remember.'

'Try to think, Miss Winter, it might be important. I've had various statements about the flare-ups at the sherry party on Friday evening. There have also been one or two independent reports of an argument later that night between Mr Kittering and Mr Sheppard, which appeared to become quite heated. Did he mention that?'

My lips were paper-dry. 'Only in passing.'

'Do you happen to know the reason for the confrontation?'

'Inspector—'

'Please, Mr Winter. It's essential I have this in your sister's own words.'

'He didn't give me any details. Neil's the one who can tell you.'

'Any comments Mr Kittering made to you could be helpful.' He paused but I only shook my head. 'Well, let's move on to this impression you had of someone hidden in the mist. Have you remembered anything further which could strengthen it in any way—a scent of tobacco—after-shave—anything like that?'

'No, it was really only an animal awareness until the twig snapped.'

'And the only person you actually saw was Mr Sheppard?'

'Later, yes.'

'Were you expecting him?'

'No, it was—quite a surprise.'

'Now think carefully, Miss Winter. How much time had elapsed between hearing that twig crack and coming face to face with Mr Sheppard?'

'It's hard to say. I started to run immediately, but I didn't know which way to go and I think I went rather a long way round. It could have been three or four minutes.'

'Time enough, in fact, for someone who did know the right direction to circle round in front of you and appear to be coming up the hill?'

'It wasn't Neil,' I said through juddering lips. 'He'd only just arrived. He told me so.'

My teeth had started rattling together and uncaring I thrust my tongue between them to still the noise.

'Did he offer any explanation as to why he should happen to be climbing the hillside in the mist?'

'He was coming to look for me.'

'In spite of the fact that he knew you were with Mr Kittering, with whom he'd had a violent quarrel the previous evening? Did he imagine he'd be welcome, do you suppose?'

'He thought I might be in danger,' I said in a whisper.

The inspector pounced. 'And why should he think that?'

'Because—it sounds silly, but—I'd told him about a dream I had of being lost on a hill in the mist. Sometimes my dreams come true.'

He frowned slightly. 'What exactly was this dream?'

'That I was looking for someone and couldn't find him.'

'That's all?'

'And I realized someone else was there and started to run away.'

'And?'—

'The mist began to thin and I saw the figure of a man turning towards me.'

'You're not trying to tell me you dreamed it was Mr Sheppard coming to the rescue?' Inspector Quiggin's voice was heavy with disbelief.

'No, in the dream the figure was part of the threat—the man I'd been running from.'

It was Martha's indrawn breath that made me realize what I'd said. For long minutes the clock ticked remorselessly into the pool of silence. Then the inspector cleared his throat and stood up. Automatically I too rose to my feet.

'Right, Miss Winter, I think that will do for the moment. If you remember anything else, however vague, you can reach me at this number day or night.' He handed me a small white card but the writing on it was a blur. As Hugo went with him to the front door, Martha put a tentative hand on my arm.

'Chloe, love—'

'I'll pour her a drink,' Hugo said tightly, coming back into the room. 'I think we could all do with one. Sit down, Chloe.' I tried to obey him but my knees were locked rigid and would not bend. I went on staring sightlessly at the card, its edges cutting into my fingers.

The drink shocked me out of my temporary paralysis and I heard myself start to laugh. 'They can't really imagine Neil had anything to do with it! It's too ludicrous for words!' Without warning my eyes were full of rushing tears. I dropped the glass on the table with a clatter and ran from the room.

For a long time, incapable of stemming the streaming tears, I stood at the uncurtained window while my double, superimposed on the dark garden beyond, wept with me. Whether I cried for Ray or Neil or myself, I had no idea.

At last I turned away and started to splash water on my swollen face. The cataclysm had calmed me and although my breath still came in long, gasping sobs, my mind was beginning to function again. Wearily I started to undress, and as I opened the wardrobe door my eyes fell on the tartan skirt hanging inside. With a sigh I ran my fingers down its soft folds, stopping abruptly as they encountered something small and hard. Memory clawed at me as I fumbled for the pocket and withdrew the silver lighter I had found beneath Ray's palette. The numbing events that had followed its discovery had completely driven it from my mind.

So I had unwittingly removed something from the 'scene of the crime' after all. In the morning I should have to phone the inspector and confess. Not that I imagined one small lighter could throw any light on the mysteries surrounding Ray's disappearance.

I turned it over in my hand and my eyes focused on an inscription on the back of it. With nothing more than mild curiosity I moved under the light to read it. In small neat lettering was engraved: *Neil from Daniel. 11.2.1970.*

CHAPTER SEVENTEEN

I slept that night with the lighter under my pillow and it permeated all my brief, tormented dreams. I shouldn't after all be phoning Inspector Quiggin; not, at least, until I had spoken to Neil. He would be able to explain how the lighter came to be on the hilltop, I assured myself endlessly, and closed my ears to the echo of his voice: *I can think of at least six people who would cheerfully slit his throat. I could myself.*

'Chloe, I'm sorry,' Martha said at breakfast, 'I have to go into college this morning. Ray's A-level class is at nine o'clock. Would you like to come?'

'I don't think so.' What I had to say to Neil couldn't be said at college. 'You'll be needing your car, then.'

'Were you wanting it?'

'I just thought I'd like to get out of the house for a while.'

'All right, I'll go in with Hugo. I should be able to persuade him to run me home at break.'

'You will be careful, won't you?' Hugo said anxiously. 'We may very well have a murderer in our midst and if he suspects that you were with Ray he might be afraid you could identify him, mist or no.'

Against my breast the little lighter lay like a lump of lead. 'I'll be careful,' I said woodenly.

As soon as the car had turned out of the gate I hurried to the phone and looked up the number of Staff House. I should just be in time to catch Neil.

'Chloe—has something happened?'

To my over-sensitive ears his voice sounded raw with strain.

'In a way. I have to speak to you. How soon can you manage it?'

'Hell, I've a very full timetable today. You're not coming in with the others?'

'No, I—I'd rather we didn't talk at college.'

'Can't it wait till this evening?'

'Not really.' Every minute could be of vital importance, to my peace of mind if nothing else. Also, I should eventually have to explain to the inspector why I hadn't contacted him at once.

'I might be able to slip out for ten minutes during the Fourth Form lesson if I set them some work, but that's not till three-thirty. I honestly can't make it any sooner; I'm even coaching in the lunch-hour.'

'That'll have to do, then. I'll wait for you at the gates.'

'Are you all right? You sound a little strained.'

'I'm all right,' I said steadily, and hoped it was true.

For once my eyes were dulled to the beauty

of the scenery as I drove down the country lanes. I turned in the direction of Andreas, principally because it was new to me and held no memories either of Neil or Ray. Memories were dangerous things that day. I met no other traffic on the road. It was almost as though the island respected my need for solitude, and the loneliest place of all was the bleak, northernmost tip of land at Point of Ayr.

I parked the car by the lighthouse and walked across the springy turf to the cliffs, where I stood gazing out across the sea to Scotland only sixteen miles away. The strong wind brought tears to my eyes and over my head the inevitable gulls dipped and soared as they had above my ledge three short days ago. But the empty spaces offered after all no escape from the doubts and fears I was trying to resolve and I returned dejectedly to the car.

I don't know at what stage I realized that I was heading for Peel and Granny Clegg. By the time it filtered through to my consciousness the decision was fully formed. Granny would help me. She had been fond of Ray and tried to warn him with her strange riddles. *Begun in September, done ere November*—and Ray had disappeared on the thirtieth of October! Could there be some solution here? What was it he had begun in September?

It was exactly one week since I had come this way with Ray. I jolted over the uneven cobbles and came to a halt outside the remembered doorway. Kirree Clegg was waiting there, her face grave, her beautiful eyes transparently troubled.

'It's yourself, then,' she said quietly in greeting. 'We've been expecting you.'

Her mother was in the huge rocking-chair as before. She nodded across to me, her beady black eyes avidly scanning my face. Did she remember giving me a feather from St Catherine's Hen, sixty years of her lifetime ago? It was impossible to guess.

'You've not had your midday meal, I'm thinking,' Kirree said matter-of-factly, and I realized with embarrassment that my arrival had coincided with lunch time. She brushed my polite protests aside and laid a place for me on the scrubbed table-top. A sizzling from the old stove in the corner and the richly appetizing smell unmistakably identified the meal as herrings. I knew that this fish had been the staple diet of the Manx for generations, and wondered how many over the centuries had sat in this little room to eat them. Martha'd told me that the Deemster's oath ended with the promise to administer justice 'so indifferently as the herring backbone doth lie in the middle of the fish'.

The meal was eaten in a comfortable silence, the fish being accompanied by bread and unsalted butter and cups of sweet strong tea. When we'd all had sufficient Kirree

217

quickly cleared the table and old Granny, her eyes for the moment unclouded, held out her tiny claw.

'There's something you've brought me, I'm thinking, that might answer your questions.'

Hesitantly I unbuttoned the neck of my dress and withdrew the lighter, warm from my flesh.

'There now. Let's be after seeing what it can tell us.'

She took it in her brown, gnarled hands and a far-away look came over her wizened little face. 'Sure, and a frightened man it was held this,' she said after a moment.

'Ray?'

'No, not himself, rest his bones. A clever man, tall and fair, knowing what he wants and meaning to get it. But there's violence there too, ugly, driving him on.'

'No!' I whispered involuntarily.

'Sure, 'tis not his fault entirely. Didn't I tell the boy his mischief-making would rebound on him?'

'But he'd never have hurt Ray!' I insisted desperately.

'You know the one I speak of?' The sharp old eyes softened. ' 'tis terrible hard, child, but I can't be changing what is done.'

Blocking off that avenue, I asked instead, 'Mrs Clegg, where is Ray?'

Her gaze shifted, took on another dimension. 'Not far away, dearie. Beneath the coloured stars.'

Hadn't she once said much the same to Ray himself?

'I don't understand,' I said plaintively. 'I want to find him.'

'Sure and you will, child, you will.' A sudden spasm shook her little body and the lighter clattered on to the table. I reached out and retrieved it, my fingers closing round it protectively. Behind me Kirree laid a warning hand on my shoulder and when I looked up she nodded towards her mother. The old woman was muttering incoherently and as the rigidity which held her melted away she began to rock gently backwards and forwards. The steady, repetitive movement had a disturbingly hypnotic effect and I remembered hearing that mental patients kept up this same mindless rocking, perhaps instinctively striving to correct their own imperfect rhythms.

'What the hell do you want?'

The voice was Ray's and I leapt out of my chair, sending it skidding across the floor. Again I felt the pressure, more insistent this time, of Kirree's hand as she righted the chair and eased me back on to it. Incredibly there were still only the three of us in the small, shadowed room. With the breath knotting in my throat I gazed fearfully at the upturned, in-looking old face across the table.

'What are you doing here?' Ray again, with a note of unease apparent now. The old woman's head was cocked as though she listened to the reply. Though her lips barely moved, the voice came over unspeakably spine-chilling, riveting myself and Kirree to mesmerized immobility.

'Oh, for God's sake! You didn't really think I'd say anything? As if it matters to me where your inclinations lie!' And then, on a note of sharp fear: 'What are you doing? Look, I'm not alone, you know. Chloe's here. She'll be back any minute now the mist's coming down. For God's sake man, be reasonable! I won't say a thing—I swear it! Get back, you bloody fool! Are you insane?' And then the urgent cry which had echoed in my head to rouse me from sleep. 'Chloe!'

We waited, motionless, and an obscene gargling sound issued from the wrinkled old throat, followed by total silence. As the force that had held her withdrew the old woman slumped forward, her hard, knobbly little chin on her flat black bosom, and a moment later, while we still stared, she began to snore.

'She'll sleep for some time now,' Kirree said in her down-to-earth voice. 'It always takes her like this.'

I wrenched my eyes away from the emptied face to the calm, plain one with its wildly improbable eyes. 'He's dead, isn't he?'

'There's little doubt of it at all.'

It was no surprise. I'd known, even before I'd returned to the deserted canvas. But to have had his last words played back so accurately—and I didn't doubt their accuracy—that was gruesome indeed. To whom had he been speaking? To a tall, ambitious man who was potentially violent? My fingers clenched on the lighter and I slipped it back into its hiding place. Now I had to go and meet Neil.

Awkwardly I opened my handbag, but Kirree reached forward and snapped it shut. 'No, no, don't think of it. Mother was fond of the boy. If she's helped you, that's enough.'

I came out of the cottage into the sunshine of Peel Harbour as if emerging from a lifetime of underground darkness. 'Are you insane?' Ray had cried, and of course the answer must be 'Yes'. Temporarily, perhaps, but undeniably, at that particular moment, insane. The coldness spreading inside me was untouched by the sun, locked away beyond the reach of warmth and light in a desolate prison of fear.

'Chloe! What on earth are you doing here?'

I spun round to see Vivian Quayle smiling at me. Her eyes went to the door of the cottage I'd just left. 'Been having your fortune told? I thought you could do that for yourself!'

'Not really.' I made a supreme effort to pull myself together. 'What about you? You're not going there, are you?'

She laughed. 'Good gracious, no! In any case, my future's looking a whole lot brighter all at once. No, I was on my way back from Castletown and thought I'd take some kippers home.' She nodded towards the old smoke houses.

'Incredible about Ray Kittering, isn't it?' she added conversationally. 'We've not had so much excitement in a long while. That's what I get for saying island life is dull! Can I give you a lift home?'

'No thanks, I have the car.'

'I'll be on my way, then. Hope your fortune was a good one!' And she clicked away along the quayside in her high-heeled shoes.

I was becoming used to the necessity of keeping my mind blank. I watched the white rise of the road in front of me, the colours of the trees overhead, the grey stone walls on either side. As I reached the gates of St Olaf's I saw that Neil was already waiting for me.

'Chloe, what is it? You look as though you've seen a ghost!'

I'd heard one, at any rate. When I did not reply he added, 'Drive along here for a hundred yards or so and you can turn into one of these farm tracks. I don't suppose anyone will be along for a few minutes.'

For seconds longer as I followed his suggestion I was able to keep my mind on the car, my hands on the wheel. Then, as the engine died into silence, no further delay was possible. I must do what I had to.

Groping towards some desperate, unformed

prayer, I retrieved the lighter, warm to my cold fingers. Without a word I handed it to Neil.

'Good Lord, where did you find this? I'd almost given up hope of getting it back! It was a twenty-first present from my brother.' He turned towards me, smiling, but at the sight of my frozen face exclaimed urgently, 'Darling, what is this? What's happened?'

I didn't allow myself to register the involuntary endearment. 'When did you realize you'd lost it?'

'About ten days ago, I suppose. Why?'

'*Ten days?*' My head snapped round to face him.

'It must be quite that. I put a notice on the board about it last week.'

Deep inside me the ice was beginning to melt. I said tremulously, 'Neil, you are sure? All that time ago?'

'Of course.' And as he continued to stare at me in bewilderment, I weakly leaned my head on his shoulder and closed my eyes. Thank you, thank you, thank you. His arm came tightly round me.

'Sweetheart, I don't begin to understand what all this is about. Why is the lighter so important?'

I took a deep breath. 'I found it on the hill, under Ray's palette.'

There was a long, measureless silence. Then: 'Are you telling me what I think you are?'

'Probably.'

'Chloe, look at me! When did you find it? Not later than Sunday, because the area was cordoned off. Why didn't you tell me before?'

'I forgot about it. I found it when I went back to the painting site in the mist. I thought Ray had dropped it, so I slipped it into my pocket and with everything else that happened I forgot all about it.'

'Until?'

'Last night. That was when I saw the inscription.'

'And you wondered whether I'd killed Ray?' There was an odd note in his voice and I didn't meet his eyes.

'Not really. I just—had to see you.'

'Have you reported this to the police?'

I did look up then. 'Oh Neil, how could I?'

'You stupid, trusting little fool!' he said roughly. 'Don't you realize the risk you were taking?'

'There's something else I must tell you,' I broke in quickly. 'I've just been to see Granny Clegg. She's a medium of some sort—Ray took me there last week.' Haltingly I related how she'd interpreted the vibrations from the lighter and the terrifying reproduction of Ray's last few minutes.

Neil took hold of both of my hands and held them very tightly. I could feel his trembling. 'There are times when you frighten the life out of me, do you know that? You go waltzing off

224

to all kinds of dubious places, gathering heaven knows what lethal information, and all the time there's somebody not too far away who knows for a fact that you were with Ray on Saturday and who may be very worried indeed that you could identify him. Hell's teeth, it could easily have been me! But no, you come trustingly to me and hand over that damn lighter for all the world as though we were at some vicarage tea-party! Don't you see how irresponsibly you're behaving? When I think what might have happened—'

He released my hands and pulled me closer. 'What am I going to do about you? You're not safe to be out alone! Heaven help me, I may have only known you—what?—two weeks, but if anything happened to you—'

He kissed me bruisingly. 'Look, will you promise me something? Go straight home, looking neither to left nor right, and phone the police immediately. Lord knows what they'll make of all the airy-fairy stuff, but give them the facts about the lighter. You'd better keep it for now, they're sure to want it. Then stay in that house and don't so much as open the front door unless Hugo or Martha is with you—preferably both of them. That ought to keep you safe for the moment. After that—' He looked down at me with a smile. 'I'm probably rushing my fences, but why not? These last few days have made me only too aware of the way I feel. It's obvious I shan't have any peace of mind until I can look after you myself, so as soon as all this ghastly mess is cleared up I intend to marry you, my girl. If you'll have me, that is, and there'd better be a damn good reason if you're thinking of turning me down!'

'I wasn't!' I said meekly.

After a few breathless minutes he looked at his watch. 'Hell and damnation—Lower Sixth Greek in five minutes! Darling, I'll have to go. It's anybody's guess what those boys will be taught this afternoon! Promise me faithfully that you'll take care. I'll be round about five and perhaps we'll be able to discuss things more calmly then.'

I backed Martha's little car out of the farm track and drove the few yards to the college gates. Then, having dropped Neil, I turned in the direction of Ballacarrick, my mind such a jumble of joy and fear that I gave up all attempt at logical thought. Which was probably why, seeing the telephone kiosk opposite the village school, I decided not to waste a moment longer in contacting Inspector Quiggin with my report about the lighter. In any case, it would be easier to explain without Martha listening in the background, full of questions.

It was after four by now, and the school was emptying rapidly, children hurrying out of the yard and along the road in search of tea and the telly. Two minutes later I was speaking over the wires to the inspector.

'Mr Sheppard's lighter, you say?'

'Yes, but he lost it ten days ago. He can prove that—there was a notice on the board about it. I just assumed it was Ray's, but now that I think of it he always used matches. And, Inspector, there's something else. I'm not sure if you'll believe me. Perhaps, as a Manxman, you just might.'

'Another of your warning dreams, is it?'

'No, not this time. I can't really explain over the phone.' Standing in my bright little capsule, I was suddenly aware of the swift approach of darkness, the now deserted school looming on my left. Belatedly I remembered my promise to go straight home.

'Very well, Miss Winter, if you think it's important I'll be with you in about twenty minutes.' The phone clicked in my ear. I put down the receiver and pushed my way out of the kiosk. Alongside me, hardly distinguishable in the deep shadow thrown by the school wall, the guy still lolled in his barrow, patiently awaiting his conflagration.

As I took a step forward a sudden explosion close at hand jerked me to a standstill. Up into the darkening sky shot the white streak of a rocket which hung poised for a moment before cascading into a shower of brightly coloured stars. Someone apparently couldn't wait till the fifth of November.

Coloured stars! My involuntary movement

227

brought me up against the barrow and the huddled form of the guy toppled slowly sideways. Automatically, my mind a riot of conjecture, I bent to straighten him and found myself staring with glazed eyes at a human hand which hung lifelessly down from the shabby black sleeve.

As Granny Clegg had promised, I had found Ray.

CHAPTER EIGHTEEN

I seemed to have been standing for ever in that colour-streaked darkness while fireworks burst all round me, spattering their garish red and green light on the dusty black figure in the barrow. Finally, with a supreme effort I uprooted my feet and, abandoning the car, set off at a shambling run along the dark lane to the cottage.

Martha had only just managed to decipher my hiccupping sobs when Inspector Quiggin arrived in response to the phone call. After that, police procedure slipped smoothly into gear. The inspector went back to the kiosk to await the arrival of his colleagues and Martha sat me down in Hugo's chair and held a glass of brandy to my shaking lips. The inspector had still not returned when Hugo and Neil arrived, commenting on the flurry of activity at the end of the lane.

Briefly Martha explained what had happened and I turned away from the horror on their faces. Neil gripped my hands. 'Darling, what possessed you to stop at the phone box? The last thing I impressed on you was to come straight home.'

I shrugged my shoulders. Whatever my motive had been, subsequent events had erased it from my memory.

Hugo said jerkily, 'It just doesn't make sense. What was the point of going to all the trouble of removing the body, only to leave it where it's bound to be discovered within the next few days? Surely it would have been much simpler to have left him where he was.'

'It might have been a delaying tactic,' Neil suggested, 'or perhaps it was only meant as a temporary measure and he intended to move him again when he got the chance. We can hardly expect whoever did it to have been thinking rationally.'

A few minutes later Inspector Quiggin returned, accompanied by the grim-faced sergeant. 'Now, Miss Winter, are you feeling better?'

'A little, thank you.'

'Then I'd like you to answer some questions as fully as you can. To go back to the beginning, where's that cigarette lighter?'

He held out a clean handkerchief to receive it. 'If you've been carrying it around all this time I'm afraid there's very little chance of finger-prints. A pity; it could have been a vital clue if you'd left it where it was.'

'I didn't know then that anything had happened.'

'I appreciate that. Now, sir.' He turned to Neil. 'Have you any idea where or when you lost it?'

'I'm afraid not. I don't smoke regularly so I didn't miss it straight away.'

'When do you last remember using it?'

'I know I had it at the Quayles's dinner party.'

'That would be Mr and Mrs Quayle of Mona Lodge?'

'That's right.'

'And when was that?'

'Nearly a fortnight ago now. The twenty-first, I think it was. I missed it the following weekend and put a notice up on the Monday morning.'

'Were any other guests there that evening?'

'We were,' Hugo put in. 'The three of us. That's all.'

'Right. Well, we'll need Mr Sheppard's prints and Miss Winter's, for elimination purposes.'

'And Mrs Clegg's,' I said. 'She handled it, too.'

'The Granny?' The inspector looked at me sharply. 'When did you see her?'

'This afternoon. I wanted to ask her

Ray was.'

'Oh, Chloe, really!' Hugo began, but the inspector raised his hand.

'Go on, Miss Winter. What did she tell you?'

'That I'd find him beneath the coloured stars.' They all stared at me blankly. 'As I came out of the telephone box someone started letting off rockets. It suddenly struck me that they were coloured stars, and that was when I—knocked against the barrow.'

'My God!' said Neil softly.

'Did she say anything else? Anything—' the inspector's mouth twitched—'that as a Manxman I might be able to accept?'

'She went into a trance,' I said expressionlessly, 'and—and played back Ray's last words, to his murderer.'

There was total silence. Then the inspector said with an effort, 'I presume no names were mentioned?'

'No. He just said, "What the hell do you want?"'

'He? Don't you mean Mrs Clegg?'

'It was Ray's voice,' I said in a whisper.

'Did you hear the other one?'

'No.' I shuddered. 'He's still alive, isn't he?'

'What else was said?'

'Something like "I wouldn't have said anything".'

'But not what about?

'"Inclinations", I think he said. I suppose it

was some of Ray's usual scandalmongering.'

The sergeant was writing assiduously in his notebook, his impassive face betraying no flicker of what he thought of mediums and their ways.

'It doesn't narrow the field much. We always assumed the motive was to silence him. Anything else?'

'He said he wasn't alone, that I was there.'

'That's what I've been afraid of all along,' Martha said in a low voice.

'The painting itself was a give-away,' Hugo pointed out.

'Not necessarily. It might have been someone who didn't know her, but not if he spoke of her by name.'

'If it was someone who knew her as Chloe, it more or less brings it down to St. Olaf's,' Neil said flatly.

'But it can't!' I burst out. 'We know them all! How could one of them be a murderer?'

The inspector smiled wryly. 'Unfortunately murderers aren't a race apart, Miss Winter. It would be much easier for us if they were. Usually they're just ordinary people going about their ordinary lives who for some reason or other are suddenly pushed too far. It's as simple as that, the line dividing them from the rest of us. That, and the grace of God.'

His eyes went round our strained faces and he cleared his throat. 'Of course, we must remember that Granny Clegg's trances, realistic as they may seem would hardly count as evidence in a court of law. They're a guideline, nothing more. Now, to return to your discovery of the body, Miss Winter. Was that the first time you'd noticed the guy?'

'No, I saw it several times when I was with Ray.' *I always feel sorry for him,'* Ray had said.

'The boys from the village have been trundling it round for a week or more to raise money for fireworks,' Hugo confirmed. 'How long do you think—?'

'I imagine the switch was made on the night of the murder, sir. If our man waited until it was dark, he would just have had time before *rigor mortis* set in. That's assuming Mr Kittering was killed straight away. The path. lab. will be confirming the time of death.'

Without Granny's clue the gruesome disguise might have remained undetected for a while longer; perhaps, I thought shudderingly, until the village children had tried to haul the supposedly straw figure on to their bonfire.

As though reading my mind, Neil said quietly, 'Thank God they didn't decide to take the barrow round this week.'

So the questions went on, routine and repetitive, and I tried to fasten my attention on them in order to hold at bay the appalling memory which was lying in wait for me. But at last the sergeant closed his notebook and the two policemen rose to their feet.

'Miss Winter, I want you to ensure that when you leave this house you have someone with you at all times. If you have to stay here alone, don't under any circumstances let anyone in. Anyone at all,' he repeated emphatically, 'however well you may think you know them. And if anyone contacts you and tries to arrange a meeting, get in touch with us at once. I think that's all for the moment. Thank you all for your co-operation. Let's hope that now we have the body, the whole unpleasant business can be cleared up without too much delay.'

'Unless you come to college with me, you'll be alone most of the time,' Martha said worriedly as the policemen left. 'I've been asked to go in full-time until they find a replacement for Ray.'

'With the doors securely locked, she's probably safer here than she would be at college,' Hugo said grimly.

'I don't see why I should be in more danger now than I was on Saturday,' I commented. 'I should be safer, since the inspector's no doubt got all of you under surveillance.'

'Good grief, do you think so? That's quite a thought! I'll have to watch my step!' Hugo winked at me, while Martha pretended not to see.

'Whether you imagine you're safe or not,' Neil said sternly, 'you do exactly as the inspector says, do you hear? Let's hope this time you really have learned your lesson.'

I remembered his words the next morning when I stood at the kitchen window watching Hugo and Martha drive off to college. Martha had promised to slip back for lunch. Apart from that, the lonely hours stretched unrelieved until five o'clock: a long time when, despite my bravado, I found my ears were constantly on the alert for approaching footsteps.

By the time Martha returned for lunch my nerves were in shreds and I'd decided that the lesser evil would be to go back to college with her. When I suggested it, however, she sounded dubious.

'It's up to you, of course, but frankly I think you're better here, if you can stick it. The atmosphere at college is absolutely appalling. Far from what you said to the inspector, I can easily imagine any one of them being the murderer.'

I shivered. 'I hope this won't go on much longer. It's a nightmare.'

'At least things seem a lot better between you and Neil. Is it too early to ask if it's serious?'

'It's not too early and it is serious. He wants us to be married as soon as this is all over.'

She jumped up impulsively and kissed me. 'That's wonderful! I couldn't be more pleased, especially as I was so afraid we'd spoiled things for you.' She pushed in her chair. 'I'll have to be getting back. Pass the time by making out a list of wedding presents!'

It was starting to rain as she drove off and by three o'clock I had to switch the light on. I had already watched a television programme, read the paper and written to my parents, but none of these occupations had claimed more than a quarter of my attention. Whatever Martha said, I should accompany her the next day. I'd had more than enough of my solitary confinement.

Across the room the telephone shrilled. Probably Neil checking up on me during break, I thought gladly. But it was Hugo's voice that spoke in my ear. 'There's been a new development, love, and the inspector wants to see us straight away. I'll pick you up in ten minutes. O.K.?'

'I suppose so. What's happened, do you know?'

'I'll explain when I see you.'

At least it would mean getting out of the house. I went to the bedroom for my mackintosh and, shrugging it on, returned to the sitting-room window to watch for the car.

The rain was becoming heavier now, drumming on the gravel path and blotting out the hill. All the glorious colour was drained from the trees, leaving them dull and drab like the painting that had been all night in the rain. An incipient sadness seeped into me and I thought for the first time of Ray's family, his sister, whose skirt still hung in my wardrobe, and his weary-faced old grandmother who had suffered a double tragedy in the last two weeks, Ray's death following swiftly on that of Tom Kelly.

I was roused from my reverie by the sound of the car. It made a U-turn to face the main road again and drew to a halt just beyond the gate. I picked up my bag and hurried out, pulling the door shut behind me. The garden gate was cold and wet beneath my fingers and I was wiping them on my mack as I ran to the car and slid inside.

'Well, what's all the panic?' I asked, reaching automatically for the seat belt. And without warning a tiny query zigzagged rapidly in my brain. Some minute difference in the mechanism of the belt, and between one moment and the next I was drenched in icy certainty. This, though almost identical, was not Hugo's car. In the same split second we rocketed forward and I spun to see the tightly smiling face of Nicholas Quayle beside me.

'You must forgive the deception, my dear,' he said in his precise voice. 'I had a feeling you might not agree to meet me in my own right.' He took the corner on two wheels and I noted despairingly that he had turned not towards Ramsey and the safety of the police station, but in the direction of Ballaugh and the lonely, stretching curraghs.

The last piece of the jigsaw fell effortlessly

into place. I had known that the tall fair man, ambitious and frightened, was not Neil. By the same token I should have known it was Nicholas. Nicholas, who had the same model car as my brother, who was a brilliant mimic; Nicholas, who for so long had been under such an intolerable strain and at whose home Neil had mislaid his lighter. My mouth was arid.

'Where are we going?' I asked.

'To the scene of the crime, Chloe, where else? Isn't it accepted that the murderer always returns there?'

'But—why?'

He didn't answer directly. 'Old Granny Clegg told you where to find him, didn't she? I'm afraid you must blame her for your present predicament. Truly, I've been bending over backwards to avoid hurting you, but when Vivian mentioned seeing you at the Cleggs', I knew it was hopeless and of course my fears were confirmed an hour or so later, when the police mustered in force outside the village school. I waited all evening for them to come and arrest me. I could hardly believe you hadn't told them.'

'I didn't know,' I whispered sickly. 'She didn't say—'

'I appreciate this must seem poor thanks for having spared me, but you see I'm too old not to be cynical. You've obviously been weighing up the pros and cons and I didn't kill Ray just to start paying out to someone else.'

'He was blackmailing you?'

'It wasn't even true,' he continued, as though I hadn't spoken. 'I swear to God I never laid hands on any boy in that way, nor wanted to. But I've been paying Ray twenty pounds a month since the beginning of term and he took that as confirmation of guilt. Of course it was stupid of me, but with the mainland appointment in the balance I couldn't afford to take chances. The merest suspicion of such a charge would have wrecked everything and Vivian had set her heart on that appointment. But in spite of the money he was beginning to make hints. You heard him yourself. It wouldn't have been long before people began to wonder.'

Since the beginning of term; 'Begun in September—'

He expertly manoeuvred the speeding vehicle past a tractor. 'Surely you agree that I was justified? I could hardly be expected to sit back and allow him to destroy me. And it wasn't only myself; he was corroding the whole college. Believe me, there will be a lot of people breathing more easily now that he's gone.'

'But I'm not a threat to anyone!'

'Unfortunately you are, since visiting the Cleggs yesterday. Why couldn't you have let well alone? You'd have come to no harm.' There was anguish in his voice, and all the time the needle of the speedometer was

239

flickering steadily upwards.

'Of course,' he went on after a moment, 'I'd intended to wait until he'd taken you home and then waylay him, but when I saw you go off alone—I'd been watching all morning through binoculars—it seemed too good a chance to miss. My car was parked out of sight round the far side of the hill and once he was dead it was a simple matter to push him over the steep face. That was for your sake, of course, to save you finding him. I believe I almost bumped into you on the way back. After you'd gone, it only took minutes to wrap him in tarpaulin and bundle him into the boot. I rather enjoyed making use of the guy—a suitably macabre touch.'

The afternoon light was thickening into rainy darkness as we sped along the narrow road and I gripped the cushion of the car seat with both hands.

'Don't be frightened,' he said rapidly, and in the uncertain light I saw that his face was shining with sweat. 'There'll be no pain, I promise. We'll just go back to the hilltop, and that's all you will know.'

I drew a long, difficult breath. So instead of simply killing me now, he intended to go to the elaborate lengths of duplicating Ray's murder. Why? Did it mean his mind had become unhinged, stuck in its own macabre groove and incapable of devising another means of disposing of me?

I said carefully, 'You won't get away with it a second time.'

'Why not?'

'I was warned not to meet anybody. I only came because I thought you were Hugo. They'll guess it must have been something like that, and only you could imitate him. And what about an alibi?'

'I said I had a dental appointment. Vivian will cover for me.'

'But the dentist won't, and they're sure to check.'

He shot me a sideways look from his pale fanatical eyes. 'I know the plan isn't water-tight—I hadn't time—'

He was actually apologizing, making excuses! I fought down hysterical laughter. 'You panicked, Nicholas. You didn't think it out carefully enough and now it's too late.'

'Vivian will cover for me,' he repeated, and added inconsequentially, 'You know, that bastard even taunted me about her.'

'She thinks the world of you,' I said gently, and marvelled at myself. Was it really incumbent on me to comfort my would-be murderer? But all at once there was something so pathetically unsure about him. I had shaken his precarious confidence and he was beginning to crumble. Ordinary people, pushed too far—

'I let her down,' he said jerkily. 'She had such high hopes when we married but I've

241

never amounted to very much. Couldn't even give her any children. And now, just when my lifelong ambition was on the point of being realized, this. It's ironic, really.'

'Take me home, Nicholas. Please. You'll only make things worse for yourself this way. You haven't a hope of getting away with it.'

The car began to swerve dangerously and I bit my lip.

'God knows I don't want to kill you but what else can I do? In time you'll put the pressure on as Ray did. You were a friend of his, after all.'

'I was sorry for him,' I said simply. 'And now, heaven help me, I'm sorry for you.'

'Don't say that!' His knuckles gleamed whitely on the wheel and as I searched for some way to calm him before he killed us both, a new sound made itself heard above the noise of our motion and the rhythmic sweeping of the windscreen wipers. It was the wailing siren of a police car. Nicholas turned wildly to look at me, seeming, I thought with compassion, about as dangerous as a frightened rabbit. Yet it was important to remember that this was the man who had killed Ray.

'Pull in to the side of the road,' I said steadily. 'They won't hurt you, I promise.'

Which was why, as the police car screamed to a halt behind us and Inspector Quiggin came running, it was to find Nicholas Quayle bent over the steering-wheel, his thin body

242

wracked with hideous sobs, while I sat unmoving beside him, my hand on his shoulder. I was wondering who would break the news to Vivian, who only the day before had laughingly told me how much brighter her future was looking.

So it was over. The threatening shadow which had haunted me across five years had come and gone. Tom Kelly was dead, and Ray too. The chain was broken and my temporary 'gift' withdrawn. For that, at least, I could be grateful. It would be many weeks before the final unravelling could take place but for the moment I had completely exhausted my capacity for fear, pity and regret. My overwhelming need was for the comfort of Neil's arms, and as the police car drew up at the cottage and he hurried white-faced to meet me, I went thankfully into them.